D1156038

FREDDY

and the

FLYING
SAUCER PLANS

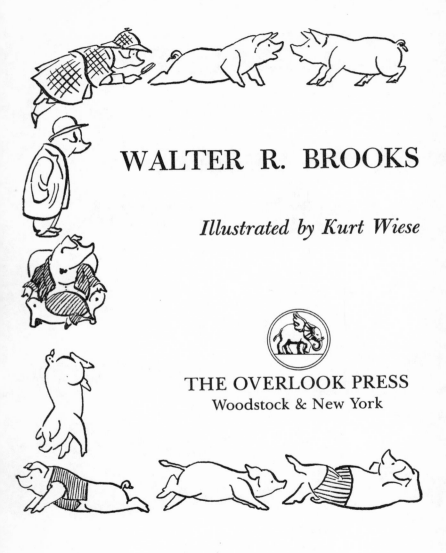

WALTER R. BROOKS

Illustrated by Kurt Wiese

THE OVERLOOK PRESS
Woodstock & New York

FREDDY

and the FLYING SAUCER PLANS

WITHDRAWN

Jefferson Madison
Regional Library
Charlottesville, Virginia

3 0470 1731

First published in the United States in 1998 by
The Overlook Press, Peter Mayer Publishers, Inc.
Woodstock & New York

Woodstock:
One Overlook Drive
Woodstock, NY 12498
www.overlookpress.com
[for individual orders, bulk and special sales,
contact our Woodstock office]

New York:
141 Wooster Street
New York, NY 10012

Copyright © 1957 by Walter R. Brooks
Renewed © 1985 by Dorothy R. Brooks

All Rights Reserved. No part of this publication may be reproduced or
transmitted in any form or by any means, electronic or mechanical,
including photocopy, recording, or any information storage and
retrieval system now known or to be invented without permission in
writing from the publisher, except by a reviewer who wishes to quote
brief passages in connection with a review written for
inclusion in a magazine, newspaper, or broadcast.

Library of Congress Cataloging-in-Publication Data

Brooks, Walter R., 1886–1958.
Freddy and the flying saucer plans / Walter R. Brooks ;
illustrated by Kurt Wiese.
p. cm.
Summary: Jinx the cat, Samuel the mole, Grisli the cannibal ant,
and the other talking animals of Bean Farm help Freddy the pig
protect Uncle Ben's flying saucer plans from greedy foreign spies.
[1. Pigs—Fiction. 2. Animals—Fiction. 3. Spies—Fiction.
4. Mystery and detective stories.]   I. Wiese, Kurt, 1887-1974, ill.
II. Title.
PZ7.B7994of   1998   [Fic]—dc21   98-41963
ISBN 0-87951-883-9

Manufactured in the United States of America
3 5 7 9 8 6 4 2

FREDDY

and the

FLYING

SAUCER PLANS

CHAPTER

1

Freddy, the pig, was sitting in a garden chair just outside the door of the First Animal Bank, of which he was president. During banking hours in the summertime he usually sat here. The banking hours were on Thursdays from two to three, the hottest part of the day; and the bank, which was just a shed at the side of the road, was like a furnace in the afternoon. But outside, under the shade of the roadside maples, it was always cool.

Freddy had on levis and boots and one of his thunder and lightning cowboy shirts; his ten-gallon hat was on the grass beside him, and he was strumming lightly on his guitar and singing one of the cowboy songs he had written when he first took up horseback riding.

Some folks think that I ought to settle down,
But I don't like the city and I don't like the
    town.
I don't like houses, I don't like walls,
I don't like bedrooms, living rooms or halls.

For a life in the open, it is gay and it's free.
There ain't any limits on the wide prairee.
And I'm goin' right back where there ain't any
    fences,
Where trouble don't begin because it never com-
    mences,
Where I can sing, yell and holler till I'm ready
    to stop,
And there ain't anybody who can go call a cop.

Cy, Freddy's western pony, was standing beside the chair. "That's a right purty song, Freddy," he said. "But for a guy that likes the wide open spaces, you sure do stick around that pig pen a lot."

"I know it, Cy," said Freddy. "We haven't been riding more than a couple of times this year. But I've been so busy—what with all the trouble the rats caused, and then before that, that flying saucer full of Martians, and the Martian baseball team we organized. And of course there's the bank here to attend to, and the *Bean Home News* to get out every week. I've taken on too much, Cy. I know it. It's more than one pig ought to try to handle.

"But I've made up my mind—I'm going to take a vacation. A nice long horseback trip—maybe we'll go West and have a look at a real prairie, instead of sitting here and singing about it. Just you and me and Jinx and Bill."

Bill was the goat. Jinx had had a saddle made for him and for a couple of summers had ridden a lot. But like Freddy, the cat had been so busy with other things that for a long time Bill's saddle and bridle had been gathering dust on their pegs in the stable.

"That sounds swell!" said Cy. "Maybe we

could get us some prize money at some of the rodeos. Enter me as a wild horse, same as we did before, hey? When we going to start?"

"Mr. Bean says it's O.K. if we go tomorrow. Jinx and I have got it all planned. Bill wants to go, and if it's all right with you . . ."

"You bet it's all right," said the pony. "This is a nice place to live, the Beans are right nice folks and so are the other animals. But sitting round in a pasture with a lot of cows isn't my idea of a rich, full life. Not that I've got anything against cows, you understand, but they aren't very exciting. —Hey, here comes Jinx now."

The cat had come out of the gate and was trotting down the road toward the bank. He had something in his mouth, and when he came up he laid it on the grass before Freddy. "Look what I found," he said. "What is it, Freddy?"

The pig leaned over and examined the little animal, which peered up at him with near-sighted eyes.

"It's a mole," he said. "Where'd you find it?"

"On the front lawn. It was—"

"I was not *on* the lawn—I was under it!" the mole said angrily. He had a small voice like a mouse, but huskier. He sounded like a hoarse mouse, if you can imagine that.

"Well, you were making a mess of it," said the cat. "Little ridges all over the nice smooth lawn. What'll I do with him, Freddy? I don't want to eat him."

"What's your name, mole?" Freddy asked.

The mole drew himself up, and recited:

Samuel Jackson is my name,
America is my nation.

The Bean farm is my dwelling place
And heaven's my destination.

"Ha, a poet he is!" said Cy with a snicker, and Jinx said: "Heaven's your destination, all right, if you dig any more holes in Mr. Bean's lawn."

"Aw, I didn't hurt your old lawn. Just little tunnels under the grass. Just little tunnels. All you got to do is stamp 'em down and your lawn's smooth again."

"Stamp *you* down and it would save a lot of work," said the cat. "Samuel Jackson, eh? The name's longer than you are."

"Well, what's the matter with that?" the mole demanded. "It's a good name, ain't it? I say, it's a good name."

"Look, mole," said Jinx, "we don't care what

your name is. Just get this through your head: Mr. Bean's lawn is out of bounds for moles. If you want to walk around on top of the grass, O.K.—nobody'll bother you. But if you walk around *under* the grass, then you'll have me to deal with. And the next time I won't be so gentle."

"Phooey!" said Samuel contemptuously. "You'd never have caught me if I'd seen you first. Can't catch me now, I betcha. I say you can't catch me now."

Jinx crouched and prepared to pounce, but before he could move, Samuel seemed to dive into the ground, making swimming motions with his big, turned-out front paws, and then he was gone.

They could see the ridge grow in length as the mole tunneled swiftly under the grass roots toward the fence. When the movement stopped, Jinx dashed to the far end of the ridge and dug into the tunnel with his claws. But it was empty. The cat hesitated a moment, looking bewildered, and then Samuel's voice behind him said: "I told you you couldn't catch me." The mole had made his tunnel and then backed quickly out of it, and now was sitting where he had been when he had issued his challenge.

"Don't call me Sammy!"

Jinx whirled. "Why, you—"

"Take it easy, Jinx," Freddy said warningly.
The cat relaxed. "Yeah," he said. "I guess
you're right. O.K., Sammy, you win. I didn't—"

"Don't call me Sammy!" the mole shouted,
flying into a rage. "Nothing makes me madder
than that silly nickname. Sammy, Sammy,
Sammy!" he exclaimed disgustedly, and each
time he said it he seemed to become more furi-
ous, so that he hopped right off the ground.

Freddy thought: I've heard of people being
hopping mad, but I never really saw anybody
hop before. He said: "Well, my name's Frederick, but everybody has always called me Freddy.
I like it."

"Well, I don't," said the mole. "If you want
to talk to me, you call me Samuel. I say you call
me Samuel."

"All right, Samuel," said Freddy. "Now let's
start all over again. What are we going to do
about you?"

"You don't have to do anything about me.
Samuel Jackson can take care of himself."

"Oh, yeah?" said Jinx. "Well, he's not going
to do it in the Beans' front yard. If you want
to eat grass roots, there's plenty of good grass

here beside the road without crawling around under a nice lawn and humping it up."

"What do you think I am, a cow?" Samuel sneered. "Moles don't eat grass, they're hunters. I say they're hunters. They pursue their prey in the dark among the grass roots, and they capture it and eat it."

"Some prey!" said the cat. He wrinkled his nose distastefully. "I suppose you mean bugs and angleworms."

"Sure he does," said Freddy. "Moles are in-sectivorous."

"Hey, you watch your language!" said the mole severely. He peered hard at Freddy with his nearsighted eyes. "You're a fine one to be calling names. What are you, anyway, in those fancy clothes—you out of a circus? I say, you be-long to a circus?"

Freddy said: "I'm a pig. I'm president of this bank, the First Animal Bank of Centerboro."

"Pig, eh?" said Samuel. "Never had much use for pigs. So you're president of this bank. Sort of a piggy bank, hey?" He doubled up with laugh-ter.

"You're only about the two hundred and eighty-fifth animal to make that crack," Freddy said. "But skip it. Yes, it's sort of like a piggy bank. You leave your money and valuables here for safe keeping. We look after 'em for you."

"Yeah," said the mole sarcastically. "I bet!"

"Sure," said Freddy, "you bring money in, and then when you want some of it, you just come in and get it."

"Sounds nice when you say it," Samuel said. "But suppose I left some money here with you. How do I know you'd give it back to me when I wanted it? I say, how do I know you'd give it up?"

"Because we give you a receipt for whatever you bring in. And we guarantee its safety. We've got safe-deposit vaults underground, and they're guarded night and day so nobody can sneak in and steal the stuff. Why, look up there!" Freddy pointed to the sign: FIRST ANIMAL BANK, under which was printed: NO LOSS TO ANY CUSTOMER IN OVER A CENTURY.

"Phooey!" said the mole. "That bank hasn't been going for a century."

"Of course it hasn't," said Freddy. "It's been going about five years. But that motto up there is the truth just the same. If we haven't lost anything in those five years, we couldn't very well have lost anything in the ninety-five years before that, because we weren't there."

"H'm," said the mole thoughtfully. "Why didn't you say: No loss to any customer for two thousand years? That's true, too, isn't it?" He turned to Jinx. "What do you know about this bank? Is this guy on the up and up?"

"Look, mister," said the cat. "How long you been living around here?"

"All my life," said Samuel. "I say all my life."

"All your life, and you don't know who Freddy is?" Jinx demanded. "I guess you don't get around much, do you?"

"Oh, I get around," said the mole. "Yeah, I guess I've heard the guy mentioned. But us moles, we don't pay much attention to what goes on above ground. Still . . ." He hesitated. "You got any money in this bank, cat? I say, you got any money in here?"

"I've got *all* my money in here," said the cat. "That's the way I feel about how safe it is. And any other animal on this farm will tell you the same."

Freddy grinned, for he knew that Jinx had just eight cents in the bank. The cat had had a good deal more than that at various times. But cats never can seem to save any money, and Jinx was a free spender; when he got a little money it trickled right through his claws.

Samuel looked thoughtful for a minute, then he seemed to come to a decision. "Maybe I could use your bank," he said. "I've got quite a little money saved up. Trouble is, I don't know just where it is."

"I don't get you," said Freddy.

"It's like this," said Samuel. "Us moles find a lot more valuable things than you'd think—things people have dropped. I remember my grandfather telling me how he found a gold watch once. Probably it fell out of somebody's pocket, and then he didn't know where he'd lost it, and the grass grew up over it and the rain washed dirt around it so that in a few years it sank into the ground. Grandpa said it was a couple inches underground when he ran on to it.

"Well, I've got some stuff I've found—money and an emerald ring and a gold pencil and so on. I suppose your bank could keep it safe for me?"

"Just bring it in," said Freddy. "We'll rent you one of our safe-deposit holes; there's just a nominal monthly rent—a cent a month and up, according to the size of the hole. They're perfectly safe from burglars—five feet underground and guarded day and night. Would you like to inspect the vaults?"

"Well, I've got to find the stuff first," Samuel said.

"Got to find it!" Freddy exclaimed. "I thought you'd found it once. I thought—"

"Let me tell my story, will you?" the mole interrupted. "I say, let me tell my story. I did find the things. But then I lost them again. A year or so ago I hid them under Mr. Bean's front lawn. And now I've forgotten where I hid them. That's what I've been doing under the lawn—hunting for them. I don't hunt for food under that lawn; there's hardly a beetle or an angle-worm left there, on account of those robins—J. J. Pomeroy and his family—that live in the big tree inside the gate. No mole could make a living there; they've stripped the place of game. You help me find my stuff and I'll put it in your bank, and then you won't have to worry about the lawn any more. I say, you needn't worry about that lawn; there won't be any reason for me to go there any more."

"You're sure it was under that front lawn that you hid the things?" Freddy asked.

"Of course I'm sure. I picked the lawn specially. Fields and gardens are no good: they get ploughed up. So do pastures sometimes. But that lawn has been a lawn for a hundred years, and will be for another hundred. My stuff's safe there."

"Why do you want to get it then?" Jinx asked. "Why not leave it there, unless you want to sell the ring or spend the money?"

"That's a silly question," said the mole. "I say that's a silly question. Sure it's safe, but it isn't really mine when I don't know where it is."

"I know what you mean," said Freddy. "It isn't that you want to do anything with it; it isn't even that you want to touch it and look at it. You just want to know where it is."

"You've got it," Samuel said. He went closer to Freddy's chair and squinted up at him. "You've got an honest face," he said. Then he caught sight of the guitar, lying on the ground. He started back in alarm. "Hey, what's this thing? Got a hole in it. Ain't a trap is it? I say is it a mole trap?"

"Oh, don't be so suspicious," said the pig. "It's a musical instrument." He picked it up and twangled a few chords. Then he put it down. "Well now, Samuel, I've got an idea maybe we can find your stuff for you. We'll try it, if you'll agree to stay out of that lawn. How about it?"

"Of course I'll agree. I don't want—" He stopped, and they all raised their heads and listened. From far away down the Centerboro road there came a series of bangs and explosions. It sounded as if a giant was popping corn.

The sounds came rapidly nearer, and as Freddy and Jinx jumped up and looked, far away down the road they saw something coming toward them. It was a black speck at first, bounding like a ball as it approached. And then it grew bigger, and they saw that it was a small station wagon, coming at tremendous speed, at such speed that it every now and then left the road entirely and bounded through the air.

"Uncle Ben!" they shouted. "Hurray, here's Uncle Ben!"

And before the words were out of their mouths, the station wagon slid to a halt in a screech of tires, and the little old man who was driving leaned out. "Howdy," he said.

CHAPTER

2

Mr. Benjamin Bean was Mr. Bean's uncle. He was a very fine mechanic. He spent a good deal of his time at the Beans', working in the shop which he had set up and equipped in the loft over the horse stable. It was here that he had made the parts for the space ship in which he and Mrs. Peppercorn and some of the animals had tried to reach Mars. Here too he had put together the small atomic engine which he had installed in his station wagon, making it probably the fastest and most powerful automobile ever constructed. Although because of its speed, and the kangaroo-like jumps which it made on the open highway, few people but Uncle Ben cared to ride in it.

The year after the space ship had been lost, a flying saucer containing a number of Martians had landed in Centerboro. The Martians were small, and had four arms and three eyes; but they were pleasant, friendly people, they had traveled for a while with Mr. Boomschmidt's circus, and had spent a good deal of time at the Beans'. They liked life on earth, and would probably have stayed much longer but for one thing. The saucer had attracted a good deal of attention. It could travel at almost the speed of light, and so would far outclass even the swiftest of modern bombers. Any nation that had even a small fleet of flying saucers could rule the world.

As soon as pictures of the Martians and the saucer, and some accounts of its flight speed, began to appear in the newspapers, spies and secret agents of every nation on the globe swarmed into Centerboro. The hotel was jammed, every rooming house was crowded, there wasn't a vacancy in any of the motels for fifty miles in any direction, and hundreds camped in tents on the fairgrounds, after the circus had gone. There were spies of every nationality, and many in very queer costumes—turbans and fezzes and long bright-colored robes. All day long the lounge in the hotel looked like a meeting of the United Nations.

The saucer, which was parked part of the time at the farm, and the rest on the Centerboro fairgrounds, was the center of a milling crowd of spies. When it left to go from one place to the other they jumped into cars and followed. They climbed all over it, banged on the door, peeked in the portholes, and mobbed the Martians whenever they went in or came out. Some of them had sheaves of big bills in their hands which they offered for "just a peek inside." Others took dozens of photographs of the Martians and the saucer from every possible angle, hoping that their governments might be able to spot something in the pictures that would give a hint of how the saucer worked.

Late one night a gang, thought to be Communists, came armed with machine guns and grenades and tried to blow in the door with nitroglycerine. Fortunately, by this time a detachment of troops had been sent by the War Department to guard the saucer, the secret of which was felt to be too important to be allowed to fall into foreign hands. The gang was discovered just as it was approaching the saucer, and all the members were captured and sent to prison.

There were so many spies that none of them was able to accomplish anything. Had there been a few, a direct attack on the saucer might have been successful. But with a hundred or more of them, each small group opposed to all the others, they were constantly falling over one another; a hundred eyes watched every move of every member of the crowd, which even by three or four o'clock in the morning was as dense about the saucer as in the daytime. And at last the Martians got tired of it. They no longer had any freedom of movement; they could never escape from the crowds which followed them everywhere. So they went back to Mars.

Before the Martians attracted so much attention, however, they had given the Beans and some of the animals rides in the saucer; they had

even shown Uncle Ben all over it and explained
how it worked. With the knowledge thus gained,
Uncle Ben had decided to build a saucer of his
own. He had at first intended to build another
space ship, like the one that had been lost. But
the saucer was much faster than the ship, and
also could move much more slowly, and even
stop in the air, so that it could be used for travel
from place to place on the earth's surface, almost
like a helicopter. The ship was only good for
interplanetary travel, whereas there were a number of ways in which the saucer could be used on
earth. By saucer, for instance, a letter mailed in
New York could be delivered in ten minutes in
London.

Unfortunately Uncle Ben had used up nearly
all his money in building the ship. So he spent
several months drawing up plans and instructions for building a saucer, and then several
more trying to interest some of the big airplane
companies in putting up the money to build it.
As long as the plans were in his head, he had no
trouble with the spies, who, now that the Martians had flown back home, didn't know that anybody on earth knew how the saucer worked. But
as soon as he began talking to the airplane companies the secret leaked out. Perhaps some of

the officers in the companies talked. But from that moment Uncle Ben was a marked man.

He began to realize that wherever he went he was being followed, at first by one man, then by a dozen, then by fifty. His rooms were searched, sometimes six or eight times a day. Before long, wherever he went, he was surrounded by a crowd; spies were everywhere; if he went into a building, faces peered at him over the edge of the roof; if he went to a movie, even if there were only half a dozen people in the place when he went in, in ten minutes there wasn't an empty seat left in the house.

Of course there was safety in numbers. One or two efforts were made to kidnap him; but if one gang tried it, there were always six other gangs lurking in the background, ready to foil the attempt. For no nation wanted any other nation to get the secret.

One evening he was walking back to his hotel in Chicago from a movie, followed by the usual crowd of spies—twenty or thirty on foot, and the rest in a string of taxis and private cars. Three men rushed out of an alleyway, grabbed him, and started to drag him toward a black car which was drawn up at the curb, with one door open. But the moment they laid hands on him, the crowd of followers surged forward. No firearms were used. With clubs and blackjacks they laid out the three assailants, and then they laid into one another. The passengers in the taxis and cars leaped out and joined the fight. Probably each gang thought it was a good idea to eliminate, at least for a few days, some of the others. For a few minutes there was a magnificent eighteen-nation free-for-all. Then suddenly, just before the police arrived, the fighting stopped. The fighters slunk away down side streets, and when the police cars rolled up they saw only a dozen or so unconscious figures lying in the road. These were put into ambulances and carried off to hospitals. But Uncle Ben had ducked out among the fighters and got back to his hotel.

He was more careful after that.

When the station wagon stopped in front of the bank, Uncle Ben snatched up from the seat a thin metal cylinder about two feet long and tossed it out of the window to Freddy. "Keep this safe," he said. "Vaults." And he pointed to the bank. Then he leaned out and stared hard at the four animals. "You good Americans?" he demanded.

"Why, you know us all, Uncle Ben," said

Probably each gang thought it was a good idea to eliminate, at least for a few days, some of the others.

Freddy. "All except Samuel, here. And he lives on the farm; he's one of us."

"Why, thanks, Freddy," said the mole. "You want us to do something, mister? I say you want us to do something?"

"Just forget me," Uncle Ben said. "You ain't seen me today. Understand? Tighter you keep your mouths shut, better you'll serve your country. Here, Freddy." He held out an envelope which Freddy took. "So long. You'll hear from me." And with a series of deafening explosions the station wagon bounded on up the road.

"Funny he didn't stop to see the Beans for a minute," said Jinx.

"Better do as he asked," said Freddy. He took the cylinder into the bank. The two squirrel guards who were sitting on the planks that covered the entrance to the vaults jumped up and stood at attention. "Gustav," said the pig, "you and Archie take this down and put it in safe-deposit hole number"—he consulted a wall chart of the vaults—"number eighteen. It belongs to Uncle Ben. We'll double the guards for a while. I'll get rabbits No. 12 and 24, and I'll also alert the A.B.I., as I believe this cylinder is important to the safety of our nation."

The A.B.I. was the Animal Bureau of Intelligence, whose director was a robin, Mr. J. J. Pomeroy.

"That Uncle Ben," said Samuel when Freddy came out, "he's not much of a talker, is he? I say he's not much of a talker."

"He doesn't usually say even that much," said Freddy.

"Practically an oration for him, what he said today," Jinx added. "What's the letter, Freddy?"

Freddy opened the envelope and took out several sheets, closely written. "My goodness!" he said. "Uncle Ben sure gets talkative enough when he gets a pen in his hand." He glanced through the sheets, then looked down at the mole. "Samuel," he said solemnly, "this is highly confidential matter. Top secret. Foreign agents would pay a lot of money to know what's written here. But I'm going to let you listen to it because I believe you're a patriotic citizen. I knew your grandfather, and a more upright and honest American I never knew. So I know you won't talk. And I doubt very much that you could be bribed into talking and betraying your government with any amount of money. Am I right?"

"Oh, yeah?" said the mole sarcastically. "I guess if you really trusted me, you wouldn't make such big talk about it. I don't want to hear your darned old letter anyway. I say I don't want to hear it." And he plunged again into the earth. But this time they watched the little ridge where he tunneled go right up to the fence and under it, and out into the field beyond.

"I thought he'd go if I talked like that to him," Freddy said. "Pretty proud, moles are. That's why I did it. I didn't want to ask him to leave; this way I figured maybe he'd be irritated and go. He's probably all right, but this is too important to take chances with. Here's the letter:

'DEAR FRIEND FREDDY:

'Please burn this letter as soon as you have read it. I have just made a deal with Interminable Motors. They will put up the money for my flying saucer—that is, for the first experimental model. They will at first make the saucer itself and some of the fittings and so on, and I will make and install the engine. However, the plans for the engine itself, which is a radically new kind of power plant, I shall not turn over to them until the model has been tested and the Air Force has agreed to buy a number of saucers, as it certainly will.

'In the meantime, I have made two sets of plans for the engine. The right set I am going to leave in the care of the First Animal Bank. None of these spies who follow me everywhere will know it is there, because I shall start for the Bean home in my station wagon at a moment's notice, and I shall leave it and drive on quickly. They will try to follow me, but no spy has a car that can keep up with the station wagon, and by the time they can locate it with their planes I shall have passed the farm and struck down to the main road and gone through Syracuse.

'The wrong set of plans I shall carry with me. Eventually the agents of one nation or another will steal it from me. This will soon become known to all the other spies, and then they will leave me alone and try to capture the set from whoever has it.

'Surrounded as I am now by these gangs of secret agents, I am unable to start work on the motor. Indeed I am unable to get a moment alone. Even in bed I am constantly being kept awake by attempts to get into the room, by footsteps and the rattling of doorknobs and tapping at the windows. If there was only one gang at work it would have had me before this. It is only the large number of groups, all constantly spying on the others, that has prevented my being kidnapped.

'It will take whatever foreign government that gets the false plans from me several months to find out that they are false. By that time the motor should have been made and tested; perhaps the Air Force may have ordered some, in which case protection of the plans will be up to the government. In the meantime, guard this set well. The only other true set is in my head.

'Hoping this finds you as it leaves me, in good health, but nervous, I am

Yours truly,

UNCLE BEN' ''

CHAPTER

3

There was a long silence after the reading of
Uncle Ben's letter. Then Freddy gave a sigh.
"Well, I guess our trip is off, Jinx. Cy, we might
as well get that saddle off—"

He stopped. There was a droning in the east,

and three planes came over the horizon. They were some distance apart, but they headed toward the Bean farm. Flying just above treetop level, they circled and dipped above the farm buildings, then went on west.

"Looking for Uncle Ben, do you think?" Cy asked.

"I do indeed," said the pig. "They'd know he had a workshop here; if they lost him they'd head for the farm."

Jinx, who had gone out into the road and was looking down toward Centerboro, said suddenly: "Listen!"

A rushing sound, louder than the droning of the planes, which had died away, came up from the east, increased to sustained roar; and then the cars appeared—dozens of them. They seemed to be coming almost as fast as the planes; they were driving very dangerously, cutting out and in and trying to pass one another on the narrow road. The first one braked sharply and pulled off the road by the bank; most of the others—there must have been thirty of them—slowed down fifty yards farther on and turned in at the Bean gate. Freddy put his hat on and pulled it down over his eyes.

Several cars drew up behind the first one. The

occupants jumped out and crowded around
Freddy. The driver of the first car, a huge man
with heavy black eyebrows that were twisted up
at the outer corners like a mustache, stood in
front of the pig and smiled. It was a terrifying
smile, although it was evidently intended to be
pleasant.

"Ha, my little friend, you are the western cowboy, no? You ride the pony, you play the music.
So? I too, when I am your age, I play the cow-
punch, I shoot the six-gun—bang, bang, bang!"

"Sure," said Freddy. "I like playing cowboy.
It's lots of fun." He realized that the man
thought he was a ten- or twelve-year-old boy
playing Wild West. He was the right size for it,
and nobody, seeing him with his hat over his
eyes, could guess that he was a pig.

"Ha, is mooch fun, surely," the man agreed.
"Tell me, you are knowing Mr. Benjamin Bean?
You maybe his littly boy?"

Jinx put a paw over his mouth to smother a
laugh. But Freddy said: "No, but I know him.
He lives here sometimes." He pointed up toward the gate.

"So? Good, good!" said the man. "I come long
way to visit him. We are old friends. Those people up by house"—he shook his head—"no good.

All wanting to steal from him something. You jump on horse—go see him, tell him meet me here, right here, ten o'clock tomorrow night, no?"

A thin man with glasses and red hair said quickly: "I too am an old friend of Mr. Benjamin Bean's. *Really* a friend," he said with a dirty look at the other man.

"That's what you say," drawled a slim man with a neat pointed beard. "Look, bud," he murmured confidentially, "tell him to ask for Mr. Penobsky at the Centerboro Hotel tonight. He'll hear of something to his advan—" But he got no further, for a fourth man pushed in and hit him on the nose.

At that the man with the glasses pulled a blackjack from his pocket and slugged the big man, and in ten seconds the rest of the men had joined the fight. Jinx ducked between the thin man's legs, jumped over a man in a turban who had just been knocked flat, and skittered through the fence; and Freddy grabbed up his guitar, scrambled on to Cy's back, and cantered up the road and through the gate.

The barnyard was full of cars, and Mr. Bean was on the back porch looking down angrily at the crowd of men who pressed up close to the railing. "I tell ye, consarn ye, that Uncle Ben ain't here," he shouted. "I ain't seen him for months."

"You're *sure* he isn't here?" one man asked. And another: "Couldn't he have come today, maybe, and you not see him?"

"Look!" Mr. Bean roared, bringing his hand down with a smack on the railing. "What kind of a lot of numbskulls and ninnyhammers are you, anyway? Don't ye understand plain English? I tell ye, he . . . ain't . . . HERE!"

Some of the men, by twos and threes, had drifted away and were poking around in the stable and the cow barn. One was even trying to crawl through the little revolving door in the henhouse. Looking at the stable, Mr. Bean saw a face appear at one of the windows of Uncle Ben's workshop. "By cracky!" he exclaimed. "This is too much!" He dashed into the house and brought out his shotgun.

The big man who had interrogated Freddy had just driven up and got out of his car. Mr. Bean went down off the porch and up to him. He just said one word: "Git!" And the man got. He went straight back to his car, got in, and whirled off down the road to Centerboro.

The sight of the gun sent the other men scurrying back to their cars. As Freddy said afterwards, they probably all had pistols in their pockets, but they had nothing to gain by starting something. If one of them pulled a pistol the sheriff would probably be put on his trail, and that would badly hamper his work as a spy.

Mr. Bean turned to Freddy, who had just ridden up. "Feller up in Uncle Ben's shop," he said. "Chase him out."

Freddy had two guns in his holsters; one was a cap pistol and the other a water pistol. Sometimes, in his detective work, he carried a real pistol; but in the ordinary run of cases, where there was not likely to be any shooting, he carried the water pistol, loaded with a generous charge of strong perfumery. For most crooks would rather face bullets than be drenched with cheap perfume—first, because if they go into hiding it's easy to smell them out, and second, because they can't stand the remarks that their friends, and even people who pass them on the street, make about how lovely they smell. For Freddy's perfume was nothing that you could get rid of by taking a few baths. It clung for weeks.

The pig jumped out of the saddle and went into the stable and up the stairs. The man who

was looking over some papers on the work bench
was the man with the neat little beard who had
been down by the bank. He turned as Freddy
appeared.

"Well, boy, what are you doing here?" he
asked.

He still thinks I'm a kid playing cowboy,
Freddy thought. Well, maybe that's a good disguise. And he said: "Oh, they let me play up
here. But what are you doing here, mister?" He
pulled out the water pistol. "Mr. Bean says for
you to come down."

The man smiled a tight little smile. "Dear
me," he said, "I suppose I should have explained
to the estimable Bean, but there was such a
crowd down there . . . You see, I'm a friend of
Benjamin's—Mr. Benjamin Bean, that is. He
asked me when I was coming by to stop and pick
up some papers from his workshop. I think these
are the ones, so I'll just take them along."

"No, you'll put them down or I'll shoot you,"
said Freddy.

"My dear little boy," said the man, rolling up
the papers to stuff them in his pocket, "you must
mind your manners. My friend Benjamin will
be very cross with me if I stop here and let a
little boy with a water pistol keep me from doing

his errand. And he will be even crosser with you. Now just let me by."

Freddy didn't know what the papers were. They couldn't be important or Uncle Ben wouldn't have left them on the bench. But this man was no friend. Probably nobody had called Uncle Ben Benjamin since the day he was baptized; the Beans and the animals called him Uncle Ben, and his friends called him Ben. So Freddy said: "Put the papers down," and pointed the gun and just touched the trigger so that a few drops of perfume sprinkled the man's necktie.

He started back and wrinkled up his nose. "Phew! What have you got in that thing? Don't do that again, boy."

Freddy kept the pistol pointed: "There's half a cup full in here. Put 'em down."

Slowly the man put the papers on the bench, but as his fingers released them he whirled and made a grab for the pig. But Freddy side-stepped and squeezed the trigger hard. A stream of perfume shot straight into the spy's face.

He gave a yell and fell back against the bench, fumbling for a handkerchief to dab at his eyes, which were badly stung by the perfume. "You

A stream of perfume shot straight into the spy's face.

wretched child," he moaned, "you've blinded me."

"Oh, no," Freddy said. "It'll wear off. But you'll smell nice for a while."

The man stumbled off down the stairs; after a minute Freddy heard a car start up and drive away.

Downstairs in his stall Hank, the old white horse, was munching thoughtfully on a mouthful of hay. He looked over his shoulder at the pig. "What's all the rumpus?" he said. "And who was that man that came down from the loft just ahead of you? My, he smelled nice!"

"You mean, you *like* that perfume?" Freddy asked incredulously. "Good gracious, I think it's awful. I keep it in my water pistol for protection. I just sprayed that man with it to get rid of him. I wonder where he lives; I bet his wife won't let him in the house."

"Well, I dunno," said Hank. "Of course I never use perfumery myself. But if I went out in society more, I should think just a drop or two on my handkerchief . . . Only of course I don't carry a handkerchief. Is there any left in that water pistol? Could you put just a smidgin on the corner of the manger here?"

So Freddy did. But he shook his head doubtfully. "I don't know what Mr. Bean is going to say," he said. "Won't surprise me if he throws you out and has the barn fumigated."

"He fumigates it every day with that pipe of his," said Hank. "And I don't think he'll notice the perfumery. I don't believe he's got any sense of smell left after smoking that tobacco for forty years."

"Personally," said Freddy, "I prefer the tobacco. But there's no accounting for tastes. Golly, I know what to get you for Christmas. A bottle of that perfume."

CHAPTER

Freddy had a pet ant named Jerry Peters, who lived in the pig pen with him. Jerry had been born and brought up in an ant hill near the henhouse. Young ants are taught just one thing: to be industrious. Even sleep, ants think, is a waste of time; and as for conversation—well, just try to get an ant to stop work long enough to tell you even what time it is.

But Jerry thought there were other things in life besides work. He felt that he had earned his keep if he worked a ten-hour week; and that's all he did work. The rest of the time he took naps, or went on exploring trips around the farm, followed by Fido, a small brown beetle which he kept as a pet. Fido was about as large as the head of a pin, but he was very faithful, and a good watch-beetle; if Jerry was asleep and a spider or grasshopper came nosing around, Fido would bark to wake him up. Of course it was a pretty small bark, and sometimes Jerry didn't hear it. Then Fido would bite his leg. The beetle's teeth were even smaller than his bark, and occasionally even they didn't wake Jerry. Then Fido would rush at the intruder, snarling viciously. This never failed. Even a caterpillar would flinch when Fido came at him.

Jerry was quite accomplished for so small an insect. Freddy had taught him to read; he would walk along the lines until he reached the end of the page, where he would wait for the page to be turned for him. He could sing, too, and knew most of Freddy's cowboy songs. Freddy would have liked to accompany him on the guitar, but of course the lightest touch on the strings completely drowned out the ant's voice. Indeed, even to hear him, unaccompanied—even for that matter to hear him talk at all—Freddy had to make a megaphone out of a cone of paper and have Jerry shout through the small end.

The other ants jeered at Jerry's accomplishments. Reading, writing, even talking—all these were classed as "the useless arts." Even jeering took time from work, and they didn't do much of it. Mostly they just pushed him aside and went on working.

So finally he left the ant hill and moved in with Freddy, who at first, of course, didn't know he was there. The atmosphere of the pig pen was much more peaceful, and at the same time more stimulating, than that of the ant hill. Everything in the ant hill was rush and hurry, with meals taken on the run and no time for, or interest in, anything but work. Whereas in the pig pen there was a pleasant air of leisure, there were pictures and books, things to look at and speculate about—as well as enough cake and cookie crumbs in the crevices of Freddy's chair to feed a dozen ants for a year.

I suppose it was Jerry's curiosity that brought

him to the pig pen in the first place. Most ants
have no curiosity; that is why they have never
got any further up in the scale of civilization.
Ants would never speculate about a pig. They
would never notice him. If he stepped on their
hill and kicked it to pieces, they would never
waste time storming at him and calling him
names; they would simply go to work and rebuild. But Jerry wondered about things. And
from wondering he took to exploring. One day
he explored the pig pen. He dined off a small
piece of angel cake he found in a crack in the
floor. He spent several days poking around in
Freddy's study, and then he and Fido moved in.
They took up residence in a dark corner under
the bed. He knew that the only thing an ant has
to fear in a house is a broom, and from the
amount of dust on the floor he felt sure that
Freddy didn't even have a broom.

At first Freddy didn't know they were there,
but then one day when the pig was reading one
of his own poems out loud to see how it sounded
(he thought it sounded swell), Jerry climbed up
on the edge of the paper and waved his feelers
at him. Freddy saw that the ant was trying to say
something, so he twisted a sheet of paper into a
cone, and holding the small end down to his visi-

tor, and putting his ear at the large end, he heard Jerry ask if he would teach him to read.

I suppose Freddy was flattered at Jerry's interest in his poems. Anyway, he fitted up a matchbox in a drawer of his desk for the ant to live in. Jerry was worried about Fido; he thought perhaps he wouldn't be allowed to keep pets. But Freddy said he didn't think the beetle would be much trouble. "As long as you assure me that he isn't ferocious," he said. And he typed a sign: BEWARE THE BEETLE, and pasted it on the matchbox.

From the barnyard Freddy rode up to the pig pen. On his desk Jerry, who had been reading page 23 of an account of Freddy's career as a detective, by Brooks, was asleep at the end of the last line where he had been waiting for Freddy to turn the page for him. Fido, a little dark speck, was asleep beside him. Freddy put the small end of the megaphone down by him and woke him up.

"I've got a job for you, Jerry," he said. "How many ant hills are there in and around Mr. Bean's front lawn?"

"Ant hills?" Jerry said. "What you going to do—take a census? Oh, I'd guess twenty, twenty-five."

Jerry climbed up on the edge of the paper and waved his feelers at him.

"I suppose these ants pretty well cover every square inch of that lawn, don't they, when they're looking for food?"

"Oh, sure. They send out exploring parties all the time. Mostly soldiers. Because the different hills are always at war with one another. They're kind of like the different tribes of Indians I was reading about in that book of yours. Boy, there have been some terrible battles on that lawn. Except—well, they don't seem to have any fun fighting. They don't put on war paint or have any war cries or anything; it's just another kind of work to them. Just a job."

"You mean they don't cheer when they win? Or sing songs or anything?" Freddy asked.

"There's one lot that have a sort of song," said Jerry. "Those big black cannibal ants that live over near the barn. They sing it when they march out on an expedition. They march in a line, all keeping step, and they sing all on one note. It goes like this:

"*Tramp, tramp, tramp, tramp, tramp, tramp, tramp.*
 Tramp, tramp, tramp, tramp, tramp, tramp, tramp.

*Tramp, tramp, tramp, tramp, tramp, tramp,
tramp.*

*Tramp, tramp, tramp, tramp, tramp, tramp,
tramp.*"

"H'm," said the pig. "Melodious, isn't it? Are there many verses?"

"Dozens. But it isn't as silly as it sounds, Freddy. They use it to scare us smaller ants. And I tell you, when you hear that song coming nearer, you're just paralyzed with fright. I suppose it keeps us from putting up a fight. Then the cannibals carry us off and either make slaves of us, or eat us."

"Well, let's forget the cannibals," said Freddy. "They kind of make my flesh creep. Now, these other ants—would they listen to you if you made 'em a proposition?"

"I guess so. If I grabbed one by the leg and held him down. But even then, only if I told him where there was more work."

"Well, look, Jerry. This mole, today—" And he told the ant about Samuel, and how he had mislaid his valuables under the front lawn. "I said I'd help him find them, and I thought these ants—some of 'em must have run on the stuff.

Of course it's in a mole hole, and—golly, I didn't think of that!—maybe moles eat ants."

"Nobody would eat an ant but another ant," said Jerry. "We're too sour."

"Sour? You mean like pickles?" The pig looked at Jerry thoughtfully. "I'm very fond of pickles myself. Oh, don't look so alarmed; you could be as sour as all get-out but there isn't enough of one ant even to register on my tongue."

"Oh, yeah?" said Jerry. "Much you know about it! Why if you were just to bite off one of my legs—" He broke off. "Hey, hey, what am I saying!" he exclaimed. "This is a pretty grisly conversation, pig. What say we change the subject?"

"O.K., but look—would you call in at these ant hills, see if any of 'em have noticed an emerald ring and a gold pencil. And some money. Some of 'em must have seen the stuff."

Jerry shook his head. "You don't know much about ants, Freddy. Suppose they have seen it. Telling me about it will be just a waste of good time to them; they'll just say 'No' and go on. Chances are they won't even listen to my question."

"Well, offer them something then. How about honey? Ants like honey."

"Sure. That might work. A jar of honey to the ant hill that finds that mole's stuff."

So Jerry went out. But in a couple of hours he was back. "Doesn't work," he said. "You know what those guys said? I stopped about six places, and they all said they hadn't run across the stuff, and then they all said the same thing: that they weren't going to send out an expedition to find the stuff if other ant hills did. They said they wouldn't enter into any competition for a prize; that was just gambling, and they didn't believe in gambling.

"Well, I argued myself blue in the face, but they wouldn't give in. They just said that all the ant hills sending out expeditions to be the first to find the stuff was a race, and a race with prizes was gambling, and ants never gamble."

"Phooey!" said Freddy. "They're awful noble."

"No," Jerry said, "they just won't take a chance on doing work that they maybe won't get paid for."

"O.K.," said the pig, "then we'll pay each ant hill that sends out an expedition, whether it finds the stuff or not. Let's say half a cup of honey per hill. That ought to keep 'em happy for a month."

So Freddy rode over to Mr. Schemerhorn's and bought a five-pound pail of honey, and then he and Jerry went around and distributed half a cup at each ant hill that agreed to send out an expedition. They didn't visit the cannibal ants. Everything went well. As they left the front yard Freddy looked back and saw long lines of ants streaming out of their holes.

"You don't suppose they'll get to fighting, do you?" he said.

Jerry was riding just inside Freddy's ear. "I doubt it," he said. "It would interfere with work. Of course one hill might raid another hill to steal the honey. Or two gangs might meet down in a mole tunnel, and if neither was willing to give way, or if one of 'em took a nip at another when they were passing each other . . . Ants have pretty short tempers, Freddy. If you interfere with them, they'll go for you. But there isn't anything personal about it; it's just because you're interrupting their work."

"But what's all the work *for?*" Freddy asked. "They don't have to work like that just to keep their ant hills in repair and get enough to eat, certainly. Don't they ever give parties, or sit around and tell stories and sing, or just wander around and look at the scenery? You do those things. But you're an ant too. You don't work all day and all night."

Jerry said: "I don't know, Freddy. I guess I just don't care enough about belonging to the biggest ant hill, or having the most food stored away, or having the record for the largest number of ant-hours put in at work per week. But the ants aren't so much different from the folks in Centerboro that you've told me about. Lots of them work harder than they have to, just so they can have as shiny a car or as nice clothes as the people next door. Keeping up with the Joneses —isn't that what you call it?"

"That's right," said Freddy. "It's just showing off. Well, me, I'd rather have more fun than the people next door, and let them have their shiny car. I don't want to keep up with anybody; I'd rather take more naps than the Joneses. Speaking of which," he added, "let's go back home and take one right now."

CHAPTER

5

Uncle Ben drove on through Syracuse westward. He saw the planes circling overhead and knew they had spotted him, but he didn't care. He had made his plan. He didn't want to hide from them yet. He drove just fast enough to keep well

ahead of the cavalcade of cars full of spies that
was pursuing him. When, looking in the rear-
view mirror, he saw the leaders coming into view
behind, he touched the accelerator and the station wagon leaped forward, thirty yards at a
bound, until they were again out of sight.

He went on through Rochester, then Buffalo,
letting his followers keep him in sight. Now it
began to grow dark. The planes had gone. Fifty
miles west of Buffalo the cars began to put their
lights on, and then he stepped on the accelerator
and quickly took a lead of three or four miles.
With nothing in sight behind him, he slowed
down, turned around, and headed back the way
he had come.

His pursuers came in sight—a long string of
glittering lights; car after car swished by without
paying him the slightest attention; for of course
they couldn't see the station wagon or its driver
—only its bright headlights. As soon as they had
all passed he speeded up; by midnight he was
back in Centerboro. He went to the hotel and
got a room and went straight to bed.

Uncle Ben had the best sleep that night that
he had had in months. There were no stealthy
footsteps in the hall, no rustlings in the clothes
closet or whisperings outside the window. But

he knew it was only a breathing space—it wouldn't last. Having lost him, in a day or two the spies would come pouring back into Centerboro, trying to pick up the trail again.

And of course he wanted them to. He didn't want to lose them entirely, because he had to manage it so that one of them would steal the false plans. He wanted to lose them just long enough to give him time to figure out what to do. Freddy was good at figuring such things out. The first thing in the morning he called up the Bean farm and asked Mrs. Bean to send Freddy down to the hotel.

It wasn't easy to talk things over with Uncle Ben, because Uncle Ben wasn't much of a talker. He hardly ever said more than three words at one time. When Freddy met him at the Centerboro Hotel he only said two: "Need help."

"Sure," said Freddy. "I read your letter. Where are all the spies?"

"Buffalo," Uncle Ben said.

"I see. You led 'em out there and then doubled back."

"Back tomorrow," Uncle Ben said.

"You mean you— Oh, *they'll* be back tomorrow," said Freddy. "I see. And then you'll be in the middle of a howling mob again. You won't

be able to go to work on the saucer until someone has stolen this"—he pointed to the metal
cylinder on the dresser—"and yet the gangs all
watch one another so closely that no one gang
can steal it. My goodness, this kind of thing can
go on for years." He scratched his head perplex-
edly. "Look here," he said suddenly, "the important thing is for you to get your plans—the real
plans—out of our vaults, and go to work building your engine, isn't it? Well, suppose I steal
this—suppose I steal it right now. As soon as I'm
gone you holler for the police. When the spies
get here, they'll hear all about it and they'll
chase me. They won't bother with you any
more. And you can go up into your workshop
and get on with the job."

Uncle Ben frowned doubtfully. "Danger," he
said. "Disgrace."

"For me?" Freddy said. "You mean they'll
kidnap me and try to make me tell where I've
hidden the plans? When they're all watching one
another, I don't see how they can kidnap me any
better than they can kidnap you. And if they do,
I'll tell 'em. That's what we want anyway—to let
'em steal this thing. As for the disgrace—well,
people will call me a thief, and maybe I'll be
arrested and sent to prison. I won't be able to

tell why I stole it and everybody will say I'm a traitor. But how else are you going to be let alone long enough to build your engine? My goodness, Uncle Ben, I don't want to sound noble, but any good American would sacrifice his reputation to get flying saucers for his country. And I'll get my reputation back, anyway, once the saucer is built and we can tell our story."

Uncle Ben argued for a while, but he had no chance arguing against Freddy, who could use fifty words to his one. Anyway, he couldn't think up any other plan. He gave in at last, and Freddy tore up one of the bed sheets and with the strips tied him into his chair, and tied a strip across his mouth. Then the pig picked up the cylinder containing the false plans. He looked critically at Uncle Ben.

"You'll do, I guess," he said. "The chambermaid will release you when she comes in to make the bed. Hold on, though. You get the state troopers in here, and they're going to wonder what you were doing all the time I was tearing up that sheet. You ought to have been yelling for help."

Uncle Ben directed his eyes down to the holstered pistols at Freddy's hips. But the pig shook his head. "Everyone around here knows one of these is a cap pistol and the other one's for water. I couldn't have threatened you with them. I ought to have knocked you out. Suppose I bang you with this thing—you've got to have a bruise to show."

But Uncle Ben didn't care for that idea, so Freddy gave it up. He thought for a minute, and then he said: "Well, then tell 'em that you were asleep and I came in and held a pillow over your face until you were unconscious." Then he picked up the cylinder and left the room.

Before he left for Centerboro that morning, Freddy had asked Jinx to stick around the pig pen, in case Jerry came back with any news from the ant hills. The cat was disappointed that they had had to postpone their riding trip, but he fully agreed with Freddy that this was no time to leave the farm. Still, he thought he could get in a little riding; he could at least pretend that they had started on their trip. So he put on his riding togs and saddled Bill and rode around the farm for a couple of hours.

It was on his fourth trip past the pig pen that he noticed an ant climbing up the door toward the keyhole. When the insect disappeared into the keyhole, Jinx dismounted, opened the door and went in. He picked up the megaphone and holding the little end down toward the ant, who was crossing the floor toward him, said: "You got a message for me, ant?"

"Are you Freddy?" the ant asked.

Jinx frowned. He was a little irritated that even an ant could mistake his slender graceful figure for the stout form of the pig.

"Freddy asked me to wait here in case there was news from Jerry," he said. "Are you Jerry?"

"Indeed I am not!" said the ant indignantly. "Even if I *am* his cousin, I hope I haven't anything in common with that lazy good-for-nothing! Lolling around under a plantain leaf all day and gossiping with ladybugs and caterpillars! Pah! I've no use for the fellow."

"Well, pah! I guess he hasn't much use for you, so that makes it even. And now what about him?"

"The cannibals have got him—that's what. He went with us when our hill started out to hunt for that Mole Treasure, as we call it. We had just gone a few yards down one of the mole tunnels when we heard very faintly behind us the cannibal marching song.

"Tramp, tramp, tramp, tramp, tramp, tramp, tramp.

Tramp, tramp, tramp, tramp, tramp, tramp, tramp.

"But it got louder and louder, and we knew they were coming down the tunnel after us. You don't know how terrifying that song is to an ant. There were forty of us, and probably not more than half as many cannibals. But if we had been at our full mustered fighting strength, five regiments, we probably couldn't have beaten them off, in that narrow space. Cannibals are five times as big as we are, and in any fight we have to win by greater numbers; it takes six or seven of us to pull down a cannibal. And there wasn't room enough for us to get at them. So we ran.

"Those tunnels branch off in all directions, and run into one another, and some of us went one way and some another; and Jerry and I and two others had bad luck: we ran down and into a dead end. There was no escape. They came after us, picked up Jerry and the two others, and carried 'em off. They missed me somehow; I was all squinched down behind a little pebble, and they didn't smell me out.

"But just as they tramped off up the tunnel, I heard Jerry yell: 'Go tell Freddy.' So—well, here I am."

Jinx knew something about the ways of ants. "Well," he said, "Jerry's gone. Why take time from your work to come tell Freddy about it?"

"We think it's part of our work. He's hired us, hasn't he?"

"I see," said the cat. "It's your duty, eh? Very commendable. H'm. I thought maybe Jerry being a relative, sort of a thirtieth cousin or something—maybe you wanted to have us try to rescue him."

The ant shrugged two pairs of shoulders. "What for? Even if we could, he isn't any good to the hill—lazy loafer!"

Jinx shook his head. "Boy, oh, boy, what an affectionate lot you ants are! Well, come on, you're still working for Freddy. Get up on Bill's neck—you'll be safer there." He went out and got into the saddle, taking the megaphone with him. "Over to that ant hill by the barn, Bill," he said.

The hill of the cannibal ants looked like a small heap of sand by the corner of the barn. The doorway was a hole beside which lounged several big ants with oversized heads and cruel-looking pincer jaws. Jinx knew that they were soldiers, guarding the gate. He dismounted and approached them. "I want to talk to your president or your king or your captain or whoever is in charge here," he said. Then he put the small end of the megaphone down toward them. "If you speak in this, I can hear you," he said.

"I'm the captain," said the biggest ant in a thin rasping voice. "On your way, cat. We have nothing to say to you."

"But I've got something to say," the cat replied sharply. "You took three prisoners yesterday. I want them turned loose, unharmed. No missing legs and feelers."

"Mister," said the captain, "we take dozens of prisoners every day. We've got 'em in the dungeons on the fifth level. You want to go down and pick out your three? Step right in." He laughed nastily, and the other soldiers cackled with him.

"H'm," said Jinx thoughtfully. "Smart guy, eh? Well, O.K., I accept your invitation. I'll come in. I'll dig 'em out." And with a sudden spring he landed on top of the ant hill and began digging frantically with his sharp claws, sending the dirt flying in all directions.

He hadn't dug very far however before the soldiers in the underground barracks rushed to the defense. They seemed to come boiling up out of the ground, big black ferocious insects, and although Jinx jumped and whirled as he dug, sending ants and dirt flying in a cloud about him, some of them managed to grab his fur, and they swarmed over him, biting until he yowled in pain, and jumping off the nest, rolled on the ground.

While Jinx was trying to get the ants off him, Bill took a hand—or rather a hoof. He plowed into the hill with all four feet, pawing and stamping and doing a lot more damage than Jinx had, and because his legs were longer and there was no fur to cling to, very few ants got on to him, and those that did, didn't bother much, because a goat's hide is thicker than a cat's.

Bill was having a good time, and the cannibal city would have been ruined for good, if Jinx, having finally got rid of his attackers, hadn't yelled suddenly: "Hey, Bill, remember Jerry is in there somewhere."

So then Bill jumped off. Jinx picked up the megaphone and went slowly closer to the hill, which was now a scene of wild turmoil. It was scooped and clawed out to a depth of nearly a foot, and soldiers and worker ants were dashing about in all directions. "Where's your captain?" he called; and when the captain came forward,

Bill was having a good time.

he said: "We mean what we say, ant. Now where are those three prisoners?"

"If it was up to me," said the captain angrily, "I'd say: go right ahead, destroy our city if you want to. We can rebuild. And then we can take our revenge. We know where you live, cat, and we can visit you there. You can watch and listen, but you have to sleep some time. That's when we'll come."

"Oh, stop talking big," said the cat. "It's not up to you anyway, you say. Well, who is it up to, then?"

"It's up to the queen. She has sent up word that if these prisoners haven't been eaten, we are to let you have them."

"Eaten!" Jinx exclaimed.

"Sure," said the captain. "When the boys get home from a raid they're hungry. They want a little snack, and they'll divide up one or two of the weakest prisoners. Good husky prisoners we keep as slaves, to work for us. But those three: I remember, weak little critters, I don't believe they've done a good day's work in their lives."

"It's just too bad for you if you've eaten Jerry," said Jinx. "You'll have Freddy on your neck, and you won't—" He broke off. "Ah, here they come," he said, as three smaller ants, guarded by two huge soldiers, appeared from one of the broken galleries of the hill. "Jerry, is that you?" And when one of the ants, coming forward through the ranks of the cannibals, who drew aside to let them pass, waved his feelers: "Climb up Bill's leg. Get on his neck and I'll take you home."

He was about to jump into the saddle when he noticed that the cannibal captain had come forward and was waving his feelers to attract attention. He pointed the small end of the megaphone down at him. "Yeah?" he said. "What is it now?"

The ant's voice came up harsh and grating, and vaguely menacing. "Just to warn you. Remember, we'll be coming up to the house to see you some dark night."

Jinx cocked his hat over his ear and waved a negligent paw. "Any time, brother—any time." And they cantered away.

CHAPTER

Freddy had his cowboy clothes on that morning, and he had ridden Cy down to the hotel. When he came out with the cylinder he jumped into the saddle and rode westward out of town toward the Bean farm. But he wasn't going home.

Once away from the town, he turned right on a dirt road that led to Otesaraga Lake.

"I hope you know where you're going, Freddy," said the horse. "We just passed two carloads of those spies—they're probably coming back to pick up Uncle Ben's trail. If you want to let 'em steal those plans—"

"If I want 'em to steal the plans," Freddy said, "we've got first to draw the whole mob away from Uncle Ben. Then when they're all chasing me, we've got to somehow let one of 'em steal them. That will take some figuring."

"Why not hold an auction," said Cy. "Golly, some of those governments would pay a couple million dollars for saucer plans, I reckon. And would you be loaded! Steam yachts and private airplanes and— Why, you could buy a ranch in Texas."

"Can't be done that way," said the pig. "I wouldn't sell even a spy false plans for money."

"You'll let him steal 'em," said Cy. "Oh, sure, there's a difference. One way you make money out of being patriotic, and the other way you're just patriotic, period. And what good is that? Sell the false plans, and you take money from the enemy. That's patriotic, isn't it?"

"Kind of hard to tell where patriotism stops

and dishonesty begins," said the pig. "Besides, how could we hold an auction? There'd just be another free-for-all fight with us in the middle of it. No, we've got to hide from the cops and then let just one spy trail us and steal this cylinder. And it's got to look good. If we make it too easy he may suspect that these plans are fakes. Then we'll be in the soup for keeps."

Indeed, Freddy didn't have any plan. As he rode along he was trying desperately to think of one. By noon he had ridden up around the east end of the lake and back along the south shore, past the estate of his friend, Mr. Camphor. He would have liked to stop in to see Mr. Camphor, but he knew that by this time Uncle Ben had given the alarm and the police would be looking for him. And if the police came, the spies would come too, and they'd be on Mr. Camphor like a swarm of bees. "It's like having the mumps," Freddy said. "You can't go near your friends for fear of their catching it too."

He found out soon enough that the police were looking for him. They'd turned up a stony dirt road that wound up into the hills, northwest of the Bean farm, and were perhaps a mile up it when behind them they heard the wail of a siren. Looking back, Freddy saw a car turning off the main road to follow them. "State cop," he said. "Darn it, he mustn't catch us. This is no time to get thrown in jail."

A couple of hundred yards up the hill the road curved and ended in the barnyard of a small farmhouse. All around were open fields. "It's the house for us," said Freddy. "There's no car around so I guess there isn't anybody home, and the front door is open. Come on, Cy. I can be the man of the house, and maybe you can get down cellar and hide." And glancing round to see that the curve of the road hid them from the trooper, he reined Cy through the barnyard and right into the front door.

They were in a hall so narrow that Freddy had to slide off over Cy's tail. There were overalls and a battered hat hanging on pegs; Freddy hung up his own hat, pulled the house owner's hat well down over his eyes and slid into the overalls. But Cy had found the cellar stairs and backed away from them. "I'm not going down there—not even to save you from the headsman's axe, Freddy," he said firmly.

Freddy didn't argue. "Up the front stairs, then," he said. "They're solid, and no cop would look for a horse upstairs."

So as Cy went clumping up to the second floor, Freddy dashed out through the kitchen. He was bending down, pulling up things in the garden that he hoped were weeds, when the trooper came around the side of the house.

"Where'd that guy go?" the officer demanded.

"What guy?" Freddy asked, wiping imaginary sweat from his forehead.

"Guy on a horse just rode in your front door."

"In the front door!" Freddy exclaimed. "Mister, you—excuse me, but you ought to wear glasses."

"I saw what I saw," said the trooper crossly. "He rode in the front door. And what's more, he didn't ride out the back door, because I was watching it. He's inside and I'm going to go in and get him." He drew a large pistol and turned back into the house.

Freddy went on pulling things up.

The trooper searched the downstairs rooms; then he went back into the hall. He opened the cellar door and looked down and shook his head. He looked at the stairs leading to the upper floor and rubbed his chin thoughtfully. "Got to be somewhere!" he muttered, and started slowly up.

"Well," said Freddy to himself, "I can't desert

Cy. He's sure to be discovered." He came back into the house and followed the trooper upstairs just as the latter, having looked through several rooms, tried a door which was locked. He shook the handle.

And from behind the door came a terrible falsetto screech, which Freddy could hardly recognize as Cy's. "Who's there?"

The trooper started violently. "Moses!" he exclaimed. Then he looked suspiciously at Freddy. "This some monkey business?" he demanded.

"It's my wife," said Freddy quickly. He spoke in a voice loud enough so that the horse could hear. Then: "Hey, Minnie," he called, "there's a policeman here looking for a man on a horse."

"Well, he ain't in here," Cy shrieked. "I'm takin' a bath, and this tub ain't no public swimmin' pool."

The trooper stepped next to the door. "I'm sorry to disturb you, ma'am," he said. His voice shook, for the dreadful screech had pretty well unstrung his nerves. "I saw them come into the house, and I thought they must be hiding here."

"And you want to look in here, hey?" Cy yelled. "Well now, you just wait a minute till I get some duds on. I'll come down and make you a nice cup of tea. You go down with pa and I'll be right along. It's always a pleasure to see new faces. —And say," Cy added, as the trooper began a hasty retreat, "I ain't seen your face yet, have I?" And with that the key turned in the lock, the door opened part way, and a terrible brown face over which a bath towel was draped, a face with an immense long nose and huge teeth showing in what was evidently meant to be a hospitable smile, appeared in the opening.

"Great Jehoshaphat Peabody!" whispered the trooper, and he fairly tumbled down the stairs.

Freddy followed him. "We don't see many folks up here," he said apologetically. "My wife gets kind of lonesome for company. We'd be pleased to have you stay for tea," he added.

But the man kept on going. "Yeah?" he said. "Well, you have my sympathy, mister." And he hurried over to his car.

After he had gone, Cy clumped downstairs. "Pretty quick thinking, eh, Freddy?" he said. "Golly, I ought to be on the stage."

"Or in the zoo," the pig replied. "That grin of yours would scare little children into fits. Hey!" he exclaimed suddenly. "The cop's coming back!" And indeed at that moment the

"Great Jehoshaphat Peabody!"

whine of an engine re-climbing the hill was re-
inforced by the squeal of a police siren.

"Upstairs, quick!" Freddy said, and made
again for the garden.

This time the trooper had his pistol out before he got out of the car. He came up to Freddy
and pointed it at him. "Go on inside," he said,
"and call your wife down. I've decided to accept
her invitation to tea."

"I wonder if you won't excuse her," Freddy
said. "She doesn't feel very well—"

The trooper grinned at him and he stopped.
"You know," the man said, "it wasn't until I got
down to the foot of the hill that it occurred to
me to wonder how come when your wife stuck
her head out of the bathroom door she had a
bridle on and a bit in her mouth." He looked
hard at Freddy. "Want to explain it?"

Freddy gave a sigh and went over and stuck
his head in the back door. "Come on down, Cy,"
he called.

So the horse came down and out into the yard.
The trooper regarded him sourly. "You're one of
Bean's talking animals, I suppose. I might have
guessed it." Then he turned and snatched
Freddy's hat off. "And you're that pig, Freddy,
the alarm is out for." He looked curiously at the

pig. "You know, in my job I have a lot to do with lawbreakers. And what I can't understand is, how folks come to be criminals. Take like you, now. I've heard about you. You've got a nicer home and a bigger reputation than any pig in the country. You've always behaved yourself and been a patriotic citizen. And all at once you steal these plans and become a thief. Not only a thief, but a traitor. I don't get it."

Freddy felt very unhappy. He didn't like being a thief and a traitor, and listening to such accusations was almost more than he could stand. But while a part of his mind was thinking this, and wishing he could tell the truth, another part was wondering how he could escape from the trooper. For it wouldn't do for him to be locked up in jail. He would be searched, and the false plans—which he had stuck down his trouser leg —would be found and returned to Uncle Ben. And Uncle Ben would be in the same old trouble again.

An hour later he still hadn't thought of anything. He was sitting in the office at the troop headquarters, being questioned by a Sergeant Candy. The trooper who had arrested him had driven off again to hunt for the plans, which Freddy described as a roll of papers about three feet long—which probably accounted for his not yet having been searched. Cy, who had trotted along behind the car, was grazing peacefully just outside the open window beside which the pig was sitting.

The sergeant had written down all Freddy's replies to questions—name, age, occupation, previous arrests, and so on. It had taken some time, for not only had Freddy been arrested several times in the past—as you probably know— but he had been, and still was, active as detective, editor, banker, and poet. The sergeant's hand got pretty tired, and at last he threw the pen down. "Don't know what use all this writing is," he said. "You admit you stole the plans."

"Oh, sure," said Freddy.

"You'll be tried for treason, as well as for stealing," said the sergeant, "and the judge will probably sentence you to life imprisonment. If you was to tell me where you hid the plans, he might knock off a few years. Save the state a lot of trouble hunting for 'em."

Freddy shook his head. He got up and went over to the window.

"Hey!" said the sergeant. "None of that! You sit down!"

"Aw, relax," said Freddy. "I'm only going to

give my horse some sugar." And as Cy came up to the window, he felt in his pocket, then held out an empty hand to the horse, who nuzzled it obligingly. Freddy put his arm around Cy's neck and his face against Cy's cheek. Cy endured these endearments with faint disgust. Freddy whispered for a moment in his ear, then gave him a pat and went back to his chair.

The sergeant got up. "Well, I guess I'd better lock you up," he said. "We'll take those pistols, and—"

Suddenly from around at the front of the building there came a series of appalling screams: "Help! Murder! Police!"

The sergeant dashed for the door, hesitating only to warn Freddy not to attempt any funny business, then was gone; and Freddy climbed out of the window, just as Cy came cantering around from the front of the house. In three seconds the pig was in the saddle and Cy was on a dead run, taking back fences with a swoop, until they were away from the town and riding cross-country, through open fields.

The sergeant, having found nothing to account for the screams at the front of the house, came back. Freddy was gone, and he ran to the window just as Cy sailed over the back fence.

They were already too far away to shoot at, so he ran out and jumped into his car.

And for a while he just sat there. For how can you pursue a horseman cross-country in a car? At last he went back in and sent out a description of Freddy to all the cars and state troop headquarters. They already had the description, but it gave him something to do. And of course he could add that when last seen, the pig was headed north.

For half an hour Cy kept on at the same dead run. Then suddenly he stopped and stood panting. "Well, Jesse James, where do we go now?" he asked.

"Gosh!" said Freddy. "I'm darned if I know!"

CHAPTER

7

While Freddy was careering around the country with the false plans, Samuel was waiting impatiently in the First Animal Bank. "A fine kind of bank president that pig is," he grumbled. "Promised to help me find my valuables, and then runs off and leaves an ant in charge of the job!''

''Look, mole,'' said Jinx, who was keeping an eye on things at the bank in Freddy's absence, ''why don't you relax? If the ants find your stuff, they'll report here and we'll go get it. How about getting some refreshments? Let's go up to the house and have a drink of milk.''

''You mean that white stuff you cats like? No thanks.''

''Well, I'll get Mr. Pomeroy to pull you a few angleworms then. You'd like that,'' said Jinx with a shudder.

''But suppose the ants have some news for me while we're away?''

''I'll get one of the dogs to come down and hold the fort,'' Jinx replied.

So they went up to the house and Jinx me-owed until Mrs. Bean set out a saucer of milk for him. Then he got Mr. Pomeroy to fly down and pull up a few angleworms for his guest. Jinx followed the robin across the lawn as he searched for worms, and the latter, who as head of the A.B.I. knew everything that was going on, brought the cat up to the minute on Freddy's activities.

''I put every available operative out in the

field as soon as Freddy alerted our office," he said. "You know my lieutenant, Horace, the bumblebee. He's in charge of a mixed crew of bumblebees and birds, following Freddy." And he told of the pig's arrest and subsequent escape. "He's still got the false plans, and he's somewhere north of Centerboro. What he'll do next, of course I don't know.

"The spies, who lost Uncle Ben somewhere west of Buffalo, are beginning to come back into Centerboro. But they've all heard about the plans being stolen, probably on the radio, and they're not after Uncle Ben any more; they're trying to figure out where Freddy is." The robin shook his head doubtfully. "I don't know. I don't know how he expects to get those plans into the hands of any one foreign government. But anyway, Uncle Ben has come out here and he's up in his shop now, hard at work."

Mr. Pomeroy had captured eight or ten fat angleworms, and he carried them in his beak over to the back porch, beside the saucer of milk. "How you can eat those things!" Jinx said. "But anyway I don't have to watch you." And he turned his back to the mole.

Mr. Bean came out on the porch. "Jinx," he said, "what's this business that's just come over the radio about Freddy stealing Uncle Ben's saucer plans?''

It shows how upset Mr. Bean was that he would ask the cat anything. Like many old-fashioned people, he became nervous when he heard animals talk.

Jinx of course didn't know anything about the scheme Freddy had cooked up. So he said: "Don't believe it. Don't believe it for a minute. Freddy's no thief."

"I dunno," said Mr. Bean. "It come over the radio—'Freddy, a pig belonging to Mr. William F. Bean, and well known and respected throughout the state.' Seems he tried to smother Uncle Ben with a pillow, and then tied him up and stole the plans. Ben says himself it was Freddy."

Jinx started to say: "But the plans Uncle Ben had—" And then he stopped. A number of the other animals had come up—Charles, the rooster, and his wife Henrietta, Mrs. Wiggins and Mrs. Wurzburger, two of the cows, and the two dogs. He felt that the fact that the stolen plans were false ones was too important a secret to mention except in confidence to one or two of the most reliable of his friends. "If Freddy did it he must have had a good reason," he said.

"I expect he *meant* all right," Mr. Bean said.

"But you know yourself, Jinx, that he usually gets in a mess when he means well."

"He usually gets out of it again," said the cat.

"Usually. But this time it's a serious crime. You don't suppose he really would sell those plans to spies, do you?"

Of course that was exactly what Freddy wanted to do, as Jinx had guessed. He didn't know what to answer. It was an unwritten rule among the animals that none of them would tell even the whitest of white lies to Mr. Bean. Fortunately at that moment they were interrupted by a cavalcade of cars that swept up the road and in at the gate. The spies had come back.

The first one that reached the porch was the dapper little man with the beard whom Freddy had squirted with perfume. He bowed to Mr. Bean. "Estimable sir," he said, "I believe you have in your employ one Freddy, a pig, an old acquaintance of mine. I have traveled many miles to see him—"

The big man with black curling eyebrows pushed up beside the speaker. "I am seeing here yesterday leetly boy in cow-punch uniform. Now I find is not leetly boy but big pig. You can telling me where is pig-house? I bring him present."

But by now the space in front of the porch

was crowded with jostling figures, all claiming friendship with Freddy, all wanting to tell him something important. Only one of them seemed to be given elbow room by common consent— the little bearded man, who still smelt dreadfully of perfume. Even Mr. Bean moved away from the part of the railing under which the man stood.

Suddenly Mr. Bean took in a deep breath. "Shut up!" he roared.

The gabble dropped to a murmur. "Yesterday you were all here asking for Mr. Benjamin Bean," he said. "You wanted his saucer plans, but he wasn't here. Well, today he *is* here, but he hasn't the plans. The radio says my pig, Freddy, stole them. Well, the pig isn't here today, and where the plans are I don't know. But one thing I do know: you're not going pokin' round in any of these buildings. You're going to get off the premises quick, immediate and pronto. Mrs. B.," he called, "bring my shotgun. Uncle Ben! Take your gun and plug the first man that sets foot on those stairs to the loft."

Jinx watched while the men slowly backed away from the porch. He saw them look up at the loft window, out of which Uncle Ben's head and the barrel of his gun were poked. But they seemed to have no interest in Uncle Ben. "They want Freddy," he thought, "because he has the plans. But what are they trying to do? Even if he was here and showed 'em that cylinder, none of 'em could steal or try to buy it. Gosh, they're stupid!"

But of course they weren't stupid. Each gang was trying to find Freddy, but each gang had also to watch the other gangs to make sure that they didn't find him and get the plans. And so they all stuck close together and watched one another.

Mr. Bean drove the men back into the cars and made them get off his property. But of course he couldn't order them off the public road, and all the rest of the day they drove up and down the road between the farm and Centerboro, and up along the back road, which ran between Mr. Bean's woods and the Big Woods north of the farm. These roads were much too narrow to handle such a lot of traffic, and the cars kept sideswiping one another. At times there were as many as eight or ten cars in the ditch between the farm and Centerboro, and farmers with tractors made quite a lot of money pulling them out. None of the accidents were serious, but many of them were done on purpose, for if some spy had a chance to push one of his rivals off the road without much damage to himself, he took it. By evening a lot of the cars looked pretty banged up.

Freddy had spent the afternoon on the edge of the Big Woods, watching the cars patrolling the back road. He had the cylinder strapped to the back of his saddle. If he could catch one car alone, he thought he might do business with it. And along toward dusk, when the traffic thinned out, he did catch one car alone. All up and down the road not another car was in sight.

When he had made sure it wasn't a state police car, he dismounted and walked boldly out into the road in front of it; then suddenly, pretending to be frightened as the car screeched to a stop, dashed back in among the trees and with one foot in the stirrup was still trying to scrabble into the saddle—without really getting into it— when the two occupants of the car caught him.

They were small, slant-eyed men—Freddy thought they might be Orientals but they spoke good English. One caught him by the arm and the other pointed a pistol at him.

"All right, Mr. Pig," said the latter. "Let's have those plans."

Freddy was perfectly willing to give them the

"All right, Mr. Pig," said the latter. *"Let's have those plans."*

plans, but he didn't think he ought to turn them over too easily. They might be suspicious. "What plans?" he said.

"Come on, come on!" said the first man impatiently. "Quit stalling." And the second man put the pistol to Freddy's ear. "I count three, then I pull the trigger," he said. "One—"

"Hey, now *wait* a minute!" said Freddy. "What'll that get you? You don't suppose I have them on me, do you?"

"I suppose we better find out," said the man with the pistol. With his free hand he slapped Freddy all over lightly. "Nothing, eh? Well, how about that tube strapped to your saddle?" And he turned toward it.

Freddy shrugged his shoulders and tried to look disappointed as he watched the man undo the strap. But suddenly he was aware that a strong smell of cheap perfume was stealing through the trees, and looking toward the road, Freddy saw that the little spy with the beard was stealing after it. He had a pistol in his fist. He pointed it at Freddy's captors and said quietly: "Put your hands up."

The men had been so intent on Freddy that they hadn't noticed the car that had slid to a stop behind theirs. Now, as their hands shot up, they swung round and saw it, and the man who threatened them. They saw also, and heard, two more cars which squealed up and stopped with a jerk.

"Oh, golly, here we go again!" Freddy said to himself disgustedly. In two minutes there were a couple of dozen spies prowling about, singly or in pairs, each watching all the others—none, apparently, paying much attention to him, although he was the center of the activity. He climbed on Cy and rode off, unmolested, through the trees.

CHAPTER

8

Freddy was pretty discouraged. At this rate no-body would ever be able to steal the plans. Yet if somebody didn't steal them, sooner or later the police would pick him up, and then the cylinder would be returned to Uncle Ben. And everybody would be just back where he started from. Except him. He'd be in disgrace. Also in jail.

Of course he could hide the things. But if it was known that he had hidden them, not only the spies but everybody in the country would go hunting for them, and he couldn't think of any place where they'd really be safe from universal search.

"Remember that money you stole once?" Cy said. "Remember where you hid it?"

"It wasn't stolen," said Freddy indignantly. "I just took it so Mrs. Bean wouldn't give it to that man who pretended to be her brother."

"O.K., so you didn't steal it," said Cy with a grin. "But when you stole it, remember where you hid it?"

"I tell you I didn't—" Freddy began crossly. Then he stopped. "Oh, sure," he said suddenly, "I hid it in the jail. Golly, that's an idea, Cy. Nobody'd look for the plans there."

"You'd be better off there yourself," said the horse. "You wouldn't have to dodge all over the country to keep from being arrested. You'd *be* arrested. And you'd get all these here spies out of your hair."

"How could I let one of 'em steal the plans if

I was in jail?" Freddy asked. "Hold on! Maybe I could, at that." He thought a minute, then he made up his mind. "Come on, Cy," he said, "I'm going down to the jail and give myself up."

Freddy managed to get to the jail, which was near the edge of town, without being observed. He rode in through the iron gates, under the archway which bore the legend:

THE CENTERBORO JAIL
A HOME FROM HOME

The lawn with its croquet wickets, mallets and balls, and its little tables shaded by colored umbrellas where the prisoners had sat drinking ice-cream sodas during the heat of the day, were deserted; it was after six, and through the dining-room windows Freddy could hear a gabble of talk and laughter and the rattle of knives and forks as the prisoners ate their supper. He unstrapped the tube of plans from his saddle and shoved it down inside his trouser leg. He gave Cy some instructions and turned him loose; then he rang the bell, and after a minute the sheriff opened the door.

He was a lanky man with a long mustache, and he had a silver star pinned to his vest. He never wore a necktie. He said that if he didn't pull it up tight it looked sloppy, and if he did, it bothered him when he wanted to swallow. He was a good friend of Freddy's, but he frowned when he saw him. "What are you doin' here?" he demanded.

"Now don't look dirty at me," said Freddy. "And you might ask me in."

"You bet I'll ask you in," said the sheriff. "And you'll stay in, too. You're under arrest."

"That's just what I want to be," Freddy replied. "Oh, don't look so sour. You'd have stolen the plans, too, under the same circumstances."

"Well, I feel sour," the sheriff said. "I got to have you here, and I suppose because we used to be friends I can put up with it. But I don't know how the other prisoners are going to feel about it. Most of our boys are good honest burglars and pickpockets and stick-up men. They ain't going to like having a traitor around any more than I am."

"Oh, for goodness' sake!" said Freddy. "I'm no more a traitor than you are. Let me in and hear what I've got to say, will you? And don't let the other prisoners see me yet."

"You're darn tootin' I won't," said the sheriff, and grudgingly led the way into his office.

"They'll likely tear you to pieces." He picked up a copy of the Centerboro *Sentinel* and read the headlines aloud.

LOCAL PIG ACCUSED OF TREASON
W. F. Bean's Freddy Steals Flying Saucer Plans
Believed Sold to Communists

"I suppose you don't deny this?"

"Certainly not. But I haven't sold 'em yet. You're going to help me do that." And Freddy grinned at him.

But the sheriff didn't grin back. "Great Jerusha!" He sounded deeply shocked and horrified. "What's got into you, Freddy? You come of good American stock, and if anybody'd asked me this morning I'd have said you was as patriotic a pig as any in the county. And now you admit the whole thing, and on top of that you're flip about it." He stared at Freddy in silence for a moment. "I just can't believe it," he said. "I can't believe you'd do such a thing. What is it, Freddy—what has happened to you?"

Freddy stopped grinning and said seriously: "I'm glad you give me the benefit of the doubt, even if it's only a little one. I know this looks bad, but we were always friends and trusted each other, and no matter how bad it looks, I hate to think you'd believe it until you'd heard my side of the story." So then he told the sheriff the whole thing.

The sheriff took a deep breath and let it out —Whoosh! Then he grinned and whacked Freddy on the back. "I ought to known—I ought to known," he said. "Yes, sir, when Ben Bean told me about how you tied him up and stole the plans, and I says: 'You want to swear out a warrant for him?'—well, Ben kind of hesitated, and then he said sort of reluctant: 'Well, s'pose I ought to.' I ought to known right then there was somethin' funny goin' on. My gosh, Freddy, if you can forgive me—"

"Forget it," said Freddy. "And now look, I suppose you'll have to put it in the paper tomorrow that you've arrested me?"

"Oh, yes. Have to. And," said the sheriff, swinging round and taking a printed form from his desk, "we might as well get you registered properly. Name? Frederick Bean." He licked his pencil and wrote it down. "Address? Bean Farm, Centerboro. Age? Well, I don't ask the boys that any more. Some of 'em are kind of sensitive about it. Feel that they're getting along in years and haven't got much to show for it, since they're still small-time burglars."

"They oughtn't to feel that way," said Freddy. "Everybody can't be rich and important. And after all, if you work hard at your job and do the best you can . . . I mean, there's nothing to be ashamed of if you haven't made a lot of money."

"That's what I tell 'em," said the sheriff. "Long as they do their best, whether it's burglary or banking, they didn't ought to be dissatisfied. Well now, let's see; here's a lot of other questions: father's name, mother's maiden name, name of dentist, number of second cousins on mother's side, unpaid grocery bills, if any . . . I don't see what that has to do with getting you into jail. Crime? What would you call your crime: assault and robbery?"

"Assault sounds kind of rough, doesn't it?"

"Well, 'cording to Ben, you tried to smother him. What'll I put—smothering and robbery?"

Freddy said that sounded all right.

"Now," said the sheriff, "what room can I give you? We're pretty full up. Having our biggest season yet. Considerin' we don't advertise in the papers—Judge Willey tells me 'twouldn't be right to advertise a jail—but considerin' we don't, we're doin' a lot bigger business than some of these summer hotels up on the lake. Of course, our charges are low, and we don't have near as many rules about behavior as they do. Having to dress for dinner and so on.

"We've got a nice bunch this season, too. All the old crowd are back—repeaters, we call 'em— and you'll see some new faces too: old Mr. Drench, he's a retired safecracker—took up passing bad checks as a hobby; and then there's the Yeglett gang, four of 'em, racketeers from the city, nice gentlemanly boys but inclined to be a little noisy at night."

All the cells in the jail were named after famous criminals, train robbers like Jesse James, or old time highwaymen like Dick Turpin. The only single cell available was Fagin, but as that had no desk in it, and no private bath, the sheriff took Freddy up to a luxurious double room, now vacant, which had not yet been named. "Maybe you could name it after me," Freddy suggested.

"I don't suppose you've got those plans on you, have you?" said the sheriff. "No, no; don't tell me now. I'll have to search you later—it's my duty. But there's no hurry. Now I wonder," he said, looking under the counterpane, "if Scarface put clean sheets on these beds. Yes, I guess so. But you'll want an extra pillow. Half a minute and I'll get it." And he left the room.

Freddy pulled the metal cylinder out from his pant leg and slid it under the mattress. He felt pretty sure that the sheriff, by going for a pillow, was giving him time to hide it. And indeed when he came back, the sheriff said: "Well, I'd better search you," and he gave the pig a perfunctory patting all over. "No, you ain't got it on you. Hid it outside, I expect. . . ." He went over to the foot of one of the old-fashioned brass beds and unscrewed the ball on top of one of the posts. "Did you know these legs were hollow? If you had that tube of plans on you, this'd be a first-class place to hide 'em. But of course you ain't." He put the ball back on.

"Well," he said, "I'll get you some supper. And by the way, some of the boys did see you as you came through the hall, so I think you'd better keep your door locked. They've heard over the radio about your stealing the plans, and there's been some pretty wild talk about what they'd like to do to you. They don't like the idea of your selling to the Communists."

"Nobody's going to like it," said Freddy, "but I've got to do it somehow. I'm not very happy about it."

He felt a little better about it a few hours later. He had had a big supper, and being tired

There was a faint scratching on the door.

from a long day in the saddle, was getting ready for bed, when there was a faint scratching on the door and a hoarse whisper said: "Hey, Freddy, lemme in."

He crept to the door. "Oh, dear," he said to himself, "I wonder if they're going to lynch me." But listening, he could hear none of the rustlings and movements that a large crowd would have made.

"Who—who is it?" he said with a quaver in his voice. The quaver made him mad and he stiffened his backbone and tried to make his tail curl up tight again—it always came uncurled when he was scared—and said in a firmer tone: "Who's there?"

"It's me, Freddy—Bloody Mike, your old pal. Lemme in, will you?"

Mike wouldn't lynch him, he thought. They had been comrades in some pretty dangerous adventures. So he unlocked the door.

The burglar came in and sat down. "Well," he said, "what's all this about you selling Ben Bean's saucer plans to some foreign spies?"

"The boys kind of mad about it?" Freddy asked.

"I'll say. They're talking pretty tough. I agreed with 'em—didn't want to get in wrong with the gang. But you know me, Freddy—I wouldn't do nothing against you no matter what you done. I thought I ought to come up and tell you to keep your door locked tonight."

"I was going to do that anyway," Freddy said.

"Yeah, well you got to watch out. Us criminals are a pretty patriotic lot of men. I expect because we're kind of easygoing in some respects, we're pretty severe in others. We have to draw the line somewhere. We'll rob and steal, but we won't have any truck with the enemies of our country. But you ain't really doing that, are you, Freddy?"

"No, I'm not," said the pig. "But I can't tell you what I really am trying to do. All I can say is, if I pull it off, Uncle Ben will be pleased. But don't tell the others."

"That's enough for me," Mike said. "And I won't tell anyone. Anyway they wouldn't believe me. But I'll try to calm 'em down."

"What were—what were they going to do?" Freddy asked.

"Well, there was some talk of tar and feathers and riding you out of town on a rail. But of course they couldn't ride you out of town, because you're in jail. And it wouldn't be very pleasant to have you around the jail all covered with tar and feathers. I don't know what they may have decided on in its place. Maybe I'd better go down and try to calm 'em down a little. Keep your chin up, Freddy. I'll stand by you."

After Mike had left, Freddy was pretty worried. Feeling among the prisoners was evidently running high against him. He had relocked the door and pushed a heavy dresser against it, and was sitting by the iron-barred window, looking out disconsolately into the night, when again there came a tap at the door.

"Freddy—are you there?"

Again he listened, and hearing no rustles or suppressed whispers, opened the door. Louie the Lug darted in.

"Hey, Freddy," he said, "you gotta watch the old step. Dese guys is out to gnaw your bones if dey can get at you. Lookit, Freddy, if youse want to get ert o' here, just gimme de woid, see? I'll stand by ya."

"You mean you don't want to tar and feather me for selling secrets to foreign agents?"

"You hoid about dat, huh? Nah, we been pals, Freddy. I know you; you ain't no traitor. I figure you got a good reason for what you done; you wouldn't do nothin' to hoit your country."

"Gee, I'm glad you feel that way, Louie," said

Freddy. "I wish the others did. Maybe some of 'em do. How about Bloody Mike?"

"Mike? Nah, he's one o' de woist ones. Said if he had his way, he'd berl ya in erl. He's de one wanted to tar and feather ya. Well, I better beat it. Remember, Freddy, I'm next door to ya on dis floor. If you want me, bang t'ree times on de wall." And he slid out.

"Well, I've got two friends here, anyway," Freddy said to himself. "I guess I have. Gee whiz, I wish Mike hadn't been the one to think up tar and feathers. And boiling in oil!" He shuddered.

And again somebody tapped on the door.

This time it was Dirty Joe, the cook. He wasn't really dirty at all; the sheriff wouldn't have let him cook if he had been. The other prisoners called him that as a joke. When a new prisoner joined them, who had never been in the jail before, they would tell him stories about how Joe never washed anything. They said he had a wash boiler hung upside down over the kitchen table, and when he had cooked a meal he put all the pans and dishes on the table and let the boiler down over them on a pulley. They said he said this kept them from getting dusty. Then when it was time to start another meal,

Joe would pull up the boiler and use all the pots and dishes over again. Usually a new prisoner didn't have much appetite for the first few days. But later, when he had seen how clean Joe kept the kitchen, he got it back.

Well, after Joe had gone, one by one nearly all the prisoners came up and tapped on the door and assured Freddy of their friendship and that they didn't believe for a minute that he was a traitor. They all said they had told nobody else, and that they had all pretended to be ready to start the lynching party at a minute's notice. Freddy felt pretty good when he finally got to bed. Maybe he and Jinx could get their trip after all. He slept like a top all night.

CHAPTER

9

Nothing much happened for a few days. The spies had learned through the radio that Freddy had been arrested and was in jail, and the Centerboro hotel and boarding houses were again full, and a dozen or more tents were up on the fairgrounds. Freddy spent most of his time in his room, watching the spies peering through the fence or peeping out from behind trees at the jail. He kept back from the window, as there was no use letting them know which room he had. He didn't go out into the grounds much either, because he hadn't yet decided which of several plans he was going to use to get the cylinder into the hands of one of the spies.

After the first day he did go down to the dining room for his meals, and though at first the other prisoners kept up the pretense of wanting to lynch him, most of them, even the newcomers who didn't know him, didn't believe that he intended to sell the plans to foreign agents. Probably because none of them would have so contemptibly betrayed their country, they could not imagine that anyone else would. Only the Yegletts, the four racketeers from the city, still scowled and sneered at him.

On the third day he was taken down to the courthouse to appear before Judge Willey. Every spy in the neighborhood attended the trial; the courtroom was jammed to the doors and many prominent local residents and friends of the accused were unable even to get inside. The Bean animals, however, were provided with seats, since they were admitted as character witnesses.

But the trial was a short one, as Freddy at once pleaded guilty to the smothering and theft charges. Since there was no proof that he had sold or even attempted to sell the plans to the representatives of any other nation, he was not even accused of treason, although there was a good deal of scowling and muttering when he was brought in, and when he stood up to be sentenced the room resounded with angry boos. Judge Willey sentenced him to five years at hard labor, but in consideration of his hitherto blameless reputation, the hard labor part was remitted. He was then returned to his cell at the jail.

Through Horace and other operatives of the A.B.I., Freddy was in constant touch with Uncle Ben and his friends at the farm. Uncle Ben had got the real plans from the First Animal Bank and was working hard at the saucer engine. The spies hadn't bothered him. One or two had been sneaking around, but as Uncle Ben had given out that the plans Freddy had stolen were the only ones in existence, and that he was now working on a new type of phonograph that would play both sides of the record at the same time, they were all now concentrating on Freddy.

This of course was what Freddy had wanted, since Uncle Ben was free to work on his engine. Life in the jail was pleasant enough; there were games to play and TV to watch and lots of good things to eat. But he couldn't go outdoors, or out for the evening with the other prisoners, and when they went to the movies he had to be content with being told about it afterwards. And as everybody knows, there's nothing duller than listening to old movie plots.

There was, too, the disgrace of being a convicted criminal, and the danger of being kidnapped and tortured to make him tell where the plans were. Naturally he would tell, but he would have to undergo a little torture to make it look good. The idea was not specially appealing. Indeed he could feel the curl coming out of his tail at the mere thought.

What he was really tempted to do was run away, and thus avoid the hatred and contempt of the townspeople and of many of his old friends. It was easy enough to do. As the sheriff said, the jail was easier to get out of than to get into. To get in you had to commit some kind of a crime but to get out, you merely told the sher-

iff that you were going downtown to buy a bag
of peanuts, or that you were invited to dinner at
Mrs. Winfield Church's. Of course he would
need a disguise to avoid the spies. But Freddy
was a past master at disguise. He had dozens of
costumes and wigs at home; all he'd have to do
was get somebody to bring him down one. Then,
when the engine was finished and the Air Force
had taken over, he could come back and tell the
true story. He liked to think about that. There'd
be banquets (for Freddy) and speeches (in praise
of Freddy) and generals presenting medals (to
Freddy).

But he couldn't do it. He had to get the plans
into the hands of one gang of spies. Until he did,
there was danger, both for Uncle Ben and himself. So he thought hard.

The spies were thinking hard too. Thinking
and lurking. They had become very good at
lurking; after the first day or two, from the jail
one could hardly ever see the lurkers, hiding behind walls and trees and bushes, watching in the
hope of locating Freddy's room by catching a
glimpse of him at a window. The only way anyone knew they were there was when one of the
prisoners would light a giant firecracker and toss
it over the fence. Then half a dozen spies would

suddenly dash from their hiding places to find cover at a distance from the explosion.

These firecrackers had been made one summer by Uncle Ben, when he was working on the exploding alarm clock which had been such a success commercially. Several of the prisoners had bought some of the crackers from him. It was of course against the law to shoot off any kind of fireworks within the city limits; there was a penalty for it of ten dollars or ten days in jail. This was just made to order for prisoners whose sentences were about to expire. They could get an extra ten days added by shooting off something. Otherwise, in order to stay in jail, they would have to go to the trouble of passing a bad check or burglarizing someone's house. In order to make it easier for them, the sheriff kept a supply of firecrackers always on hand, which he sold to them for a nominal sum.

But though the spies lurked and thought, neither activity brought results. Not until the slender man with the small neat beard had an idea. It was probably the first idea that any of the spies had had. Mostly they just hung around and watched for Freddy and hoped they could get him alone in a dark cellar where they could bang him on the head until he told them where

Then half a dozen spies would suddenly dash from their hiding places to find cover.

he'd hidden the plans. This gave them lots of time to think, but their thinking was a pretty poor grade of thinking and until this man—Penobsky was his name—had his idea, nothing that was worth trying had come to the surface.

Penobsky realized that his idea wasn't a very good one, but it was all he had, and so he acted on it. He had lived in America a good many years. When he was twenty he had joined the Communist party, more because red was his favorite color than for any other reason. Also he liked to go to meetings and applaud. It made him feel that he belonged to something.

This is a very important feeling to have, but it would have been better for him if he had joined something whose purposes he understood, like Rotary or the Salvation Army. After a while he began to feel this dimly himself. So having saved a bit of money—he was a plumber, which is a well-paid profession—he went abroad to find out.

When he came back a few years later he didn't know any more than he had before. But the Communists had supposed that he knew what they were up to because he was so enthusiastic, and so they didn't try to explain. It is always a lot of trouble to explain something that you don't understand yourself. And—because it is always easy to be enthusiastic about something you don't understand—Penobsky kept right on being a Communist.

Also he had been offered a job as a spy. And as he felt that this was a step upward in the social scale, he put away his plumber's tools, washed his face and hands, grew a small neat beard, and took it.

Penobsky knew from watching the jail that the sheriff and a good many of the prisoners always went to the local ball games. But he had never seen Freddy leave the jail. On the Saturday after he got his idea, the Tushville team was coming over to play a double-header against Centerboro. He shaved off his beard, bought a secondhand bag of plumber's tools, put on a pair of dirty overalls, rubbed a lot of black grease into his hair and over his face and hands, and walked boldly up to the jail and rang the bell. None of the other lurking spies recognized him, so they didn't interfere.

"Sheriff asked me to stop by," said Penobsky to Louie the Lug, who opened the door. "Leak in the hot-water line."

"I don't know nuttin' about it," said Louie.

"It's in the bathroom," said Penobsky.

"There's twenty bat'rooms in dis jail, chum,"
Louie said. "Dis ain't no cheap flea bag. Every
guy's got his own private bat'room, even sheriff's
got one."

"O.K., your highness," said Penobsky, "let's
see 'em all."

So Louie showed him through the jail. He
went into all the bathrooms and turned faucets
on and off and whacked pipes with a hammer.
Most of the prisoners weren't home; those that
were said they didn't have any leak. He didn't
stay long in any of the bathrooms; he was looking for Freddy, and at last he found him.

Freddy was lying on his bed, reading. He said
he felt it was his duty to read during his spare
time, to improve his mind. He was reading a
book on the lives of famous bandits. Of course
some books improve the mind more than others.
There was a tap on the door and he said: "Come
in," and Louie brought in the false plumber.
"Dis guy's lookin' for a leak in de hot water."

"Haven't got any leak," said Freddy.

Penobsky had recognized Freddy immediately. "Better be sure," he said, and started for
the bathroom.

"But I tell you—" Freddy began. Then he
stopped and wrinkled up his nose. "Perfume!"

he thought. "That's the terrible perfume from my water pistol. How could this guy . . . Golly, if he shaved off his beard and dirtied his face . . ." Then he said: "Come to think of it, there is a little leak, back of the tub. Better take a look."

As Penobsky passed the bed to go into the bathroom the smell came stronger. This was certainly the spy he had squirted with perfume in Uncle Ben's shop. Freddy thought furiously for a minute. "If I was in his place, what would I do? I guess I'd get rid of Louie, and then I'd tie me up and twist my arm until I told him where the plans were. Yeah, only I don't want my arm twisted. And if I just handed 'em to him, he'd smell a rat."

His thoughts were interrupted by a call from the plumber. "Boy, I'll say you've got a leak!" And as they looked in the door, sure enough, water was squirting out of the hot-water faucet and hitting the ceiling. "Better go down cellar and shut off the water," Penobsky said to Louie, "or we'll flood the jail."

"Louie, you stay right here," Freddy said. He had no intention of being left alone with a probably cruel and merciless spy. On the other hand, the spy must somehow be kept from leaving. For an idea had come to Freddy and he thought it might work. He said to Louie: "This guy isn't a plumber. Not if he doesn't know enough to shut off the water before he takes a faucet off."

"If dere ain't any leak, he makes one," Louie said. "Maybe he is a plumber at dat—wants to make a job for himself." Louie was smarter than he looked.

"I think he does, and he wants to make it in my bathroom because he's after me," Freddy said. "He's a spy. So let's lock him up until the sheriff gets back."

So they shoved Penobsky into the room named Fagin, and then, having turned off the water, went up and put Freddy's faucet on.

In the cellar, while turning on the water again, Louie said: "Hey, Freddy, you don't suppose dat plumber guy will escape t'rough de window, do you?"

The sheriff liked to please his prisoners, and so although there were iron bars on all the windows, he had had them fixed so the whole frame, bars and all, swung outward. He did this because the bars made some of the prisoners nervous—they said they made them feel shut in. Of course it looked all right from the outside, but as the sheriff knew, it's not pleasant to feel that you're shut in and can't get out. It was very thoughtful of him.

"He doesn't know about the windows," Freddy said. "But anyway he won't try to escape; if he'd wanted to he'd have pulled that gun on us that was sticking out of his pocket."

So when the sheriff came home Freddy took him up to see the prisoner.

The sheriff looked at him with distaste. "He's pretty dirty," he said. "What charge you expect me to hold him on?"

"Impersonating a plumber," said Freddy promptly.

"I *am* a plumber," Penobsky said and showed them his union card.

"Well, then," the sheriff began. He obviously didn't want to have this greasy and grimy creature in his nice clean jail.

"Carrying concealed weapons," said Freddy. And he slid a fore-trotter into the man's pocket and pulled out a pistol.

The sheriff said reluctantly: "We-ell, I s'pose if he'll take a bath. And wash out the tub afterward—"

"I can't take a bath," said Penobsky. "Against doctor's orders." He was afraid Freddy would recognize him if he washed his face. He didn't know of course that the pig had spotted him by the perfume.

"Well, you can't stay in my jail unless you do," said the sheriff.

"It's honest dirt," the man retorted.

"Well, there ain't any place for honesty in a jail. So we'll just let it go down the drain. I'll give you a choice; either you take a bath, or I'll have the boys give you one. With yellow soap and a scrub brush."

"There ain't any bathroom with this room," said the man sullenly.

Here was the opportunity that Freddy had been watching for. He looked meaningly at the sheriff. "He can use my tub if he'll scrub it out. And if he'll mop up the mess he made in there monkeying with the hot-water faucet."

The sheriff said all right, and when Penobsky had gone into Freddy's bathroom and shut the door, the pig took the sheriff out into the hall. "Look, sheriff," he said, "don't give this guy that single room. Put him in my room, there's two beds there."

"Got one of your ideas, hey?" said the sheriff with a grin.

"Yeah," said Freddy. "If it works I'll tell you about it in the morning."

CHAPTER
10

It took Penobsky several hours to degrease himself, and he still looked streaky. But he cleaned
up the tub and the floor before he came out of
the bathroom. He still smelt faintly of the terrible perfume, though now he was quite recog-

nizable as the dapper spy, even without the beard. But Freddy pretended not to recognize him, and asked him questions about various kinds of plumbing fixtures—which of course he knew all about.

Freddy gave him no chance to try to get information out of him by torture. The water pistol was in its holster and he kept his hand on it as they talked. Penobsky eyed it warily; it was plain he didn't want another squirt from it.

Finally Freddy said: "As soon as it's dark, what do you say we sneak out of here?"

"Sneak out!" Penobsky exclaimed. "Out of a jail?"

"Sure," said Freddy. "Look." And he went to the window and swung out the frame in which the iron bars were set. "We just drop out and beat it."

"For Pete's sake!" said the spy, who of course didn't know much about the Centerboro jail. "You known about this all the time?"

"Just noticed it this morning when I leaned on it. Well, what do you say?"

But the spy shook his head. "No, I guess not," he said. "They can't do anything to me. You see, I got a permit for that gun. If I run away I won't get it back, and the sheriff might catch up with me and then he'd really have something on me. He'll have to let me out in the morning when I show him the permit."

"Why didn't you show it to him when he pinched you?" Freddy asked.

"Do you know," said Penobsky, looking surprised, "I never thought of it! Now can you beat that for absent-mindedness?"

If he did have a permit, Freddy knew perfectly well why he hadn't shown it. He wanted to be locked up here, close to the saucer plans. But he didn't say any more.

At supper the spy was introduced merely as a plumber who had been jailed for carrying concealed weapons. He was quiet and didn't talk much, and afterwards went up to the room. Freddy stayed down playing games until bedtime. When he went up Penobsky was in bed, blinking and yawning sleepily. But his eyes didn't look sleepy.

Finally Freddy went to bed. He turned the light out, but he didn't pull down the shade, and the street light outside lit up the room so that they could see each other clearly. They lay on their sides, each in his own bed facing the other. The water pistol was in plain sight on Freddy's pillow, and he held it pointing straight at the spy. Penobsky, however, appeared not to see it. He lay with his eyes closed, and pretty soon he began to snore. So Freddy began to snore too.

Freddy lay quite still and snored. At first they were good full-bodied snores that would have done credit to someone five times as big. But gradually they grew softer and softer and finally stopped. But Penobsky's snores went on.

Then suddenly they stopped too. "Ha," thought Freddy, "he's waked up. If he really was asleep. Now's the time for my sleep-walking stunt."

Every now and then Mr. Bean would have a spell of walking in his sleep. Once he had come out late at night in his night clothes and had dashed about the barnyard, banging on the doors of the stable and the cow barn and the pig pen and the other buildings, and shouting: "Get up! To arms! The British are coming!" The animals thought he'd gone crazy, of course, and none of them let out a peep; but Mrs. Bean had come out in her old blue bathrobe, and instead of yelling at him, had gone quietly up to him and put her hand on his arm and said: "Better come back to bed, Mr. B." And he had gone as quietly in.

He didn't remember anything about it the

next morning, but he said at breakfast that he had dreamed something about being Paul Revere.

Freddy had remembered that, and another time when he had heard a noise in the night and had looked out and seen Mr. Bean, in his long white nightshirt and the nightcap with the red tassel, walking across the barnyard with his eyes shut and his arms held straight out in front of him, he had gone out and said quietly: "You'd better go back to bed, Mr. Bean." And Mr. Bean had turned around and gone, still with eyes shut and arms stretched out.

So now Freddy got up, and without trying to be specially quiet or anything, with his fore-trotters held out in front of him and his eyelids nearly shut so that he could just see, walked around the room a couple of times, muttering to himself, then went to the post at the foot of Penobsky's bed where the plans were hidden, unscrewed the knob, and took them out.

So far the spy hadn't moved or raised an eyelid. So Freddy went on muttering, only louder. Holding the tube out in front of him, he wandered about the room, saying: "Oh, dear, where shall I hide it?—What shall I do with it?—Oh, dear, oh dear, someone will find it. What can I do?—What will Uncle Ben say?—Oh, dear, if these spies get it . . ." He gabbled faster and faster and louder and louder, but the spy's eyes remained tight shut and he breathed evenly and deeply.

So then Freddy tried one last thing. He put the tube behind a picture on the wall, so that the ends stuck out in plain sight beyond the frame. "There, I guess it's safe now," he said in his gabbling voice. "Nobody'll find it there—none of those spies will get it now." He walked around Penobsy's bed twice, saying this, and then got into bed again. And began to snore.

And nothing happened. Freddy snored for half an hour, until it hurt his nose and he had to stop. But Penobsky never moved. Freddy said to himself: "The darn spy has really been asleep all the time!"

Well, there was no use going through the performance again. If the man was to witness it, he had to be awake. But how could he be waked up? Freddy couldn't do it, and then start right in sleepwalking.

He was trying to figure out some plan, when with a high, thin whine something flew past his ear, and then landed between his eyes, and

With his fore-trotters held out in front of him.

walked on tiny feet down toward the end of his nose.

"Hey, mosquito!" Freddy whispered.

"Thought you were asleep," said the mosquito. His voice was so small that Freddy could hardly hear it. "Not that it matters much. You couldn't hit me if you tried."

"I don't intend to try," said Freddy, although he couldn't keep his nose from twitching nervously as he felt the mosquito shift his feet. "But don't start drilling yet. I need your help. I want to make a deal with you."

"O.K., state your proposition. But while you're talking, mind if I take a little sip?"

"You're darn right I do! Quit it!" As he felt the tip of the stinger press his skin he spoke louder than he had intended, and Penobsky stirred uneasily. "I've got something to do," he said in a lower tone, "and I don't want to have to scratch my nose in the middle of it."

"O.K.," said the mosquito resignedly. "But hurry up. I'm thirsty."

"Well," said Freddy, "I suppose you're a good patriotic American?"

"You bet your chin whiskers I am!" said the mosquito warmly. "A hundred per cent. Why, the blood of governors runs in my veins."

"The blood of . . . What are you talking about?" Freddy demanded.

"It's gospel truth," the mosquito replied. "My home is in Albany. That's the state capitol. The governor lives there."

"I suppose you're related to him, hey?" Freddy asked derisively.

"You might say I am. I called on him one evening. I bet he paid more attention to me than he does to most of his callers."

"You bit him?"

"Once on the wrist and once on the neck. If that doesn't make us blood relations I don't know what would."

"Guess you're right, at that," Freddy said. "But let's get back on the subject. Look, I want to wake up this guy in the other bed."

"Well, go ahead. What's stopping you?"

"I want you to do it, because . . ." And Freddy explained.

The mosquito shook his head—at least Freddy thought he did, because he had to look cross-eyed to see the end of his nose, and the light was so dim that he really could hardly see the insect. "Uh-uh. You say this man's a spy? It takes away my appetite just to look at him. Anyway, do you think it is right to ask me to mix my blood with

that of a foreign agent? I'm a good American.
How do I know that won't turn me into a Communist?"

"I realize that I'm asking you to make a sacrifice," Freddy said soberly. "But is even so great a sacrifice too great to make for your country?"

"Maybe—maybe not," said the mosquito. "Come right down to it, what has my country ever done for me except try to squash me? Deny me the right to make a living? Try to slap me whenever I sit down to a meal?"

"It has supplied you with a lot of well-nourished, full-blooded subjects," said Freddy. "Suppose you'd tried to make a living in a Communist country. They don't get enough to eat—miserable, thin-blooded creatures. You wouldn't have the plump, graceful figure you have now if you lived there."

"Really?" said the mosquito in a pleased voice. "You think I look nice? Nobody ever said that to me before. Except Sanford, of course. And he don't count."

"Sanford?" Freddy asked.

"My fiancé. Goodness, I wonder if I'll ever see him again!"

Freddy said: "Your fiancé! Oh, sure." He had forgotten what of course he knew perfectly well

—that it is only the female mosquitoes that bite. He had laid on the flattery just on the general principle that most insects are pretty vain. It worked better than he had hoped.

"He's still in Albany," the mosquito said. "I got shut in a truck that was coming up to Centerboro. If Sanford had been with me it would have been all right, because it doesn't matter much where we live. But he was late for our date that night—as usual—and we weren't out hunting together, and when they opened the truck doors here I was in Centerboro. So I thought maybe the jail would be a good place to get a bite."

"Very sound idea. Well now—what's your name, by the way?"

"Sybil."

"Well now, Sybil, I'll tell you what I'll do. If you want to wake this fellow up, I'll try to get you back to Albany. Is that fair enough?"

Sybil said she thought it was, but she wasn't sure she wanted to go back. "Albany's all right," she said, "but—well, I like the country. You know how it is—you live in a city about so long and then it's enough."

"I'm afraid I don't know," said Freddy. "I've never lived in a city. But how about Sanford?"

He thought it was too bad that these two loving hearts—though small—should be separated by an unsympathetic truckman.

"Oh, Sanford!" said the mosquito. "I don't think I was ever really in love with him. Oh, well, of course if Sanford was to come up here . . . But anyway you probably wouldn't be willing to go up to Albany and get him."

"I wish you knew your own mind better," Freddy said. "But anyway, yes—if you'll wake this fellow up, and if I succeed in what I want to do, I'll go up to Albany. But how I'm to find one mosquito in a city that size—"

"I can tell you how to find him," said Sybil.

"All right, then; do your stuff."

But the mosquito now wasn't sure she could wake Penobsky up. "Most people that sleep as sound as he does," she said, "they scratch the bites in their sleep. They don't wake up at all."

"Then bite him where he can't reach it," said Freddy. "Look, his back isn't under the covers. Bite him between the shoulder blades. He'll have to wake up to reach that."

So Sybil flew over. But in a minute she was back. "He's got on pajamas that are too thick. I can't get through the cloth."

"They're some the sheriff lent him," said

Freddy. "Let's see; how about his nose—just in-side where it's good and sensitive? That ought to do it."

"Oh, fine!" said the mosquito. "And suppose he sneezes?"

"Oh, for goodness' sake," said Freddy; "a fine patriot you are! If he sneezes he wakes up, doesn't he? You want to do a fine patriotic act only you don't want to risk anything. O.K., go on, fly out the window, beat it! A big help you are to your country!"

"Oh, shut up!" said Sybil crossly. "I'm go-ing." And with a shrill whine she rose from the pig's nose and flew toward the other bed.

There was silence for perhaps twenty seconds. Then Penobsky gave a terrific sneeze, following which he sat up in bed and began furiously scrubbing the end of his nose.

"There goes Sybil!" Freddy said to himself.

He waited for a few minutes while the spy at-tended to his itching nose, then when Penobsky lay down again, and before he could get to sleep, Freddy got up. With fore-trotters outstretched and eyes shut he made for the tube. He took it from behind the picture, and muttering: "I must find a safer place for the plans—I must put them where the spies can never find them—oh dear, oh dear, where shall I hide them?" he went again through his sleep-walking routine, wandering about the room, while through slitted eyelids he watched the spy.

And this time Penobsky got up. Evidently he knew how to deal with sleepwalkers. He got quietly out of bed and came close to Freddy, without touching him. "There, there," he said soothingly, "I'll take care of them for you. I'll find a safe hiding place where the spies can't get them. Just give them to me and go back to bed and to sleep."

So Freddy handed over the tube, and then he got back into bed and pulled the covers up about his ears. But he watched. Penobsky dressed hurriedly, and with one backward glance at his apparently sleeping roommate, went to the window, swung open the frame with the iron bars set in it, and dropped quietly to the ground. And then Freddy turned over and really went to sleep.

CHAPTER

11

In case he got the plans, Penobsky had made careful arrangements for his getaway some time before. Passing himself off as an artist named Smith, he had rented a house not far from the small farm where Freddy had taken refuge from the state trooper. The huge lawn sloped away gradually on all sides from the house, and there was a clear view for a hundred yards in all directions—not a tree or bush stood anywhere within the high iron fence that surrounded it. There were three other men living there—one of them was the big fierce man with curled-up eyebrows. One always stayed with the house while the others were out spying.

Penobsky knew that even if he got the plans, it was going to be hard to get them out of the country. Not only because the spies of the seventeen other nations who were after them would be on his trail, but because the U. S. Government would be watching all the seaports and airfields as soon as it was known that he had them. But the main thing was to get them, and to keep them afterwards. Then he could wait until a good opportunity came to get away. He had plans for that, too.

The only thing he hadn't been able to plan for was how to get away from the jail unseen by the other spies. And he didn't. Cautious and quiet as he was, dozens of eyes, peering from behind trees and peeping through bushes, spotted him at once, and there was a general rush for the gate, which was the only exit from the grounds.

With the plans actually there, there would probably have been a terrible free-for-all fight, in which indeed the plans might have been destroyed. Cy, saddled and bridled, was drowsing under a tree near Freddy's window, as Freddy had asked him to. Realizing what had probably happened, and fearing that this man might not be able to escape, he trotted out. Penobsky ran to him, jumped into the saddle, and with a rattle of hoofs they were through the gate, scattering the spies like a bunch of chickens and knocking two of them endways. And then they were galloping up the empty steet while the spies ran for their cars.

Once outside the town, Penobsky made cross-country for his house, and the lights of the cars died away behind them. He kept on steadily for an hour, crossing several roads, even cantering for a mile or so along one stretch, until pursuing car lights made them take to the fields again. When finally they came to the house, Penobsky pulled up in the gateway and gave a peculiar whistle. At once a searchlight on the porch was turned full on him. Cy blinked in the glare. Then the light went off and somebody called out something in a strange language. Penobsky dismounted, gave Cy a whack on the flank and said

"Go home," and started up the drive. So Cy went back to the jail.

In the morning, Freddy told the sheriff the whole story. "I don't think we ought to say anything about it though," he said. "If they were the real plans, getting them back would be a cinch, because Cy knows where this spy is, and the state cops could besiege the house, and make him surrender. But we don't want to get them back. They'd be given to Uncle Ben, and then the whole business would start over again, with the spies and everything."

"Spies are mostly gone this morning," said the sheriff. "Mike threw a firecracker over the fence after breakfast and didn't flush one of them."

"Sure. They saw the plumber escape. They're after him now, and that's fine. But look, sheriff; that mosquito—I'm kind of worried about her. She did a fine patriotic act, and I haven't heard a peep out of her. Suppose she got hurt when the guy sneezed?"

"She may have been blown into a corner somewhere," said the sheriff. "Why don't we get the vacuum cleaner and see if we can pick her up?"

But Freddy thought that might be dangerous. "Suppose she's injured. I wish you'd help me look for her. She took a big risk—really, you know

if you or I had done that, they'd have given us
the Congressional medal."

"Well," said the sheriff dryly, "I can't imagine
doing it in the first place, and in the second, what
would she do with the medal? Hang it round her
neck? However, I'll say this: if we find her she'll
get a free meal in this jail any time she asks for
it, and no fly swatters."

It isn't easy to find a mosquito in a large room
when you want one—not that you usually do.
But the strange thing was that they did find Sybil.
She had been blown by the sneeze under Penobsky's pillow, and when they lifted it, there she
was, lying on her side and moaning feebly. She
had a broken wing.

The sheriff got a match box and put cotton in
it, and then they put the injured mosquito in it.
They couldn't of course set the wing, but the
sheriff looked at it under a magnifying glass and
said he thought it would heal all right. He gave
her some breakfast, and then leaving her resting
comfortably went down to his office.

"What I'd like to do, sheriff," said Freddy, "is
get away for a while, until Uncle Ben has his
engine made and can clear my good name. How'd
this be. Jinx and I have been planning a riding
trip, and we'll go. You give out that you're keep-

ing me, as the perpetrator of a dastardly crime against my country, in solitary confinement in the dungeon under the jail."

"There isn't any dungeon, Freddy," said the sheriff. "Goodness, you ought to know that I wouldn't have any such horrible place to stick my boys into."

"Well, and I won't be in it, either, so that's all right," said the pig.

"Eh?" said the sheriff. "Oh, I get you. On bread and water?"

"No," Freddy said. "People could imagine me in a dungeon, but they couldn't imagine me living on bread and water. Not with my appetite. No, regular meals; but no light, except what filters through a tiny barred window, high up in the damp and slimy walls."

The sheriff shivered. "Rats?" he asked.

Freddy thought a minute. "No," he said, "I think not. Snails."

The sheriff shivered again. "I feel terrible for you, Freddy," he said.

"So do I," replied the pig. "We must both remember that I won't be there. . . . Well, I'd better escape tonight, if it's all right with you."

"Some of the boys will be going to the movie tonight," said the sheriff. "Better wait till after midnight. They go early, but some of 'em stay right through the second show, and then they go get a soda afterwards. But they're usually in by twelve."

Freddy didn't say anything about all this to Horace, the bumblebee, or to any of the other operatives of the A.B.I. who came during the day to collect information or take back any messages he might have for his friends. The fewer animals or people that knew that he was no longer in the jail, the less trouble it would be for everybody.

That night, back at the Bean farm, the four mice—Eek and Quik and Eeny and Cousin Augustus—went to bed at nine o'clock in their cigar box under the stove. And behind the stove Jinx curled up on his red cushion. But nobody slept well, for Cousin Augustus tossed and turned and disturbed the other mice, who squeaked their protests; and then from muttering, Cousin Augustus began talking, so that what he said could be understood.

The mouse's voice wasn't loud enough to keep Jinx awake, but what annoyed the cat was the things Cousin Augustus said. He was calling some cat all the insulting names he could think of. Jinx knew quite well that the insults weren't meant for him; he was on the best of terms with all the mice. He just didn't like to hear any cat—even an imaginary one—called names by a mouse. To sit quietly and listen to it was in his opinion not dignified.

He got up and went over to the cigar box, with the intention of lifting Cousin Augustus out and giving him a good shaking. But in the dim light from the kerosene lamp which Mrs. Bean always left turned down on the kitchen table, the four mice looked so innocent and helpless, all lying spoon fashion in the box with Cousin Augustus in the forward position, eyes tight shut and whiskers twitching as he muttered his insults, that the cat grinned and got over being mad. He just carefully shut the lid of the box and went back to his cushion. The mice would be all right, he knew; the lid had holes in it so that in winter if the kitchen fire went out, it could be closed down and they would be warm and could still breathe.

Now it was lucky for Jinx that he hadn't gone right to sleep. He wouldn't have heard something that he did hear. It was very faint—hardly more than a whisper in the still air of the kitchen.

Tramp, tramp, tramp, tramp, tramp, tramp, tramp.

Tramp, tramp, tramp, tramp, tramp, tramp, tramp.

It was the marching song of the cannibal ants.

Jinx was off his pillow in a bound and he threw open the lid of the cigar box and shook the rearmost mouse by the shoulder. This of course shook all the mice and they awoke immediately—all except Cousin Augustus, who snapped his teeth and kicked out with all four legs—imagining, I suppose, that he was being attacked by the dream cat.

"Wake up, boys, and scatter," said the cat. "Trouble coming. But it's aimed at me, not you. Better go into the parlor. It's the cannibal ants. They said they'd get me, and they're out to do it." He stopped and pointed to a thick black line that seemed to have been drawn from the keyhole of the back door, up the wall, and halfway across the ceiling toward the stove. Another black line was creeping slowly forward across the floor.

"Golly, Jinx, don't let those ants get you or they'll eat you alive," said Quik; and Eeny said: "They've divided. That gang is going to drop on you from above, and the others are going to attack from the floor. Come on, Jinx; let's get out of here."

But the cat only grinned. "Stick around, mice," he said. "I'm going to give these boys a tonic—liven 'em up a little." His gun belt was beside the cushion—in it were duplicates of the weapons Freddy carried; a cap pistol and a water pistol. He pulled a bottle out from under the cushion and filled the water pistol from it.

A strong and sickly sweet smell of cheap perfume filled the air. The mice began to sneeze. "Get under the table, boys," Jinx said. "You ain't smelt anything yet."

Ants haven't very good eyes. They learn about the world by smelling of things and touching them with their feelers. So the cannibals, as they massed together on the ceiling above the cushion, preparing to drop on Jinx, didn't see that he wasn't there. Nor did the column that was approaching across the floor realize that he was not in his accustomed place. So when he pointed the water pistol at the mob on the ceiling, and squeezed the bulb, they were taken completely by surprise. The thin stream of perfume hit them and then traveled along the line of march, across the ceiling and down the wall to the keyhole. Then he quickly reloaded from the bottle and sprayed the entire length of the column on the floor.

"Wake up, boys, and scatter," said the cat.

The whole ant army was thrown into complete confusion. Most of the ants on the ceiling dropped to the floor and lay there kicking or trying to wash the terrible perfume off their faces with their forelegs—for if its effect on Penobsky had been so powerful you can imagine what it would be on a creature as tiny as an ant. Jinx reloaded his pistol again, but the army was in no condition to carry on an attack. They spread out over the floor, kicking and sneezing; many of them were scrambling toward the door. The cannibals were in full retreat.

But Jinx knew the grim doggedness of ant nature. They would never give up. They would be back—if not tonight, then some other night. Eek came out from under the table, holding his nose with one paw, and pointed this out. "What are you going to do, Jinx?" he asked. "You can't squash a whole army."

"Certainly not," the cat snapped. "Not when I've already licked them. I've got an idea. You boys want to come with me—over to the ant hill?"

"What!" Eeny squeaked; and Cousin Augustus said: "What's the idea? You want us to be eaten alive?"

"Look," said the cat, "every soldier in that hill came along on this expedition. They've never tackled anything as big as a cat before, and they'd be fools if they didn't bring the full strength of their army. I'll bet there isn't more than half a dozen soldiers left at the hill, to guard the gate and look after the queen's safety. O.K., let's snatch the queen. What do you say?" He got up on the table where he could reach the door knob, turned it, and opened the back door.

"Yeah!" shouted Quik. "Sure, cat; we're with you!" Eek and Eeny chimed in. But Cousin Augustus said: "Well, I'm not going. Those cannibals—if one of them bites you and you cut his head off, he goes right on biting. One bit me once—I've still got the scar. Look at it, down by the end of my tail."

"Aw, you've shown it to us about a hundred times," said Eeny, and Quik said: "Couldn't even see it with a microscope."

Eek said angrily: "It's mice like you, Gus, that give the whole mouse nation a reputation for being sissies. This army can't get back to the hill for at least half an hour, and we can get there in five minutes. Now you come along and no more nonsense, or I'll put a scar on your tail that'll really show."

So Cousin Augustus went along, but he grumbled a good deal.

It was easy enough, as Jinx had thought. A swift attack with the cat's claws scattered the few guards, and then Jinx dug down to the queen's apartments, a foot or so down. The moon gave enough light for animals to work by. Here there were only laborers, and nurses for the queen's children. The queen was big, much bigger than even the largest of her soldiers. Jinx scooped her out with a claw, and then Quik grabbed her, and carried her back to the kitchen. And it was just as they were looking for a safe place to put her that Freddy walked in.

CHAPTER

12

Freddy came quietly in the kitchen door, closed
it behind him, then stopped, sniffing the perfumed air and looking around suspiciously.
There was no one in sight; Jinx and the mice
were in the pantry, looking for something to shut

the queen up in, and the last cannibal soldier, groggy with perfume, had stumbled out under the door. "That spy wouldn't have come here," Freddy thought. "And yet that smell . . ."

Jinx, who had heard the door, came in from the pantry. "Hi, Freddy. Boy, have we been having a time!"

"It certainly smells like it," said the pig. "Has that spy been here?"

"Spy? What spy? No, the cannibal ants were here. They made a raid on us, and I drove 'em off with this." He slapped the water pistol. "So then we snatched their queen. Show him, Quik."

The mouse brought her out and put her on the floor.

"H'm," said Freddy. "If a cat can look at a king I suppose a pig can look at a queen. Not that it's any pleasure; she's no pin-up girl. What you going to do with her?"

"Make 'em promise to lay off me if I give her back. But I thought you were in jail."

"I don't want anybody to know I'm not," Freddy said. "But I thought, until we can give out the true story why I swiped those plans, you and I could sneak off and take that trip. Get clean away from Centerboro where nobody will recognize me. Start now, and by sunup we'll be twenty miles from home."

Jinx was delighted with the idea and he went off to round up and saddle Bill, and to get the saddlebags which Mrs. Bean had made for him, and which had been packed and in readiness for a week. Freddy and the mice took the queen up to the pig pen and shut her in the drawer of his desk where Jerry Peters lived. She was too big to escape through the hole that Jerry used as a door, and Jerry promised to look after her and see that she got enough to eat. Being an ant, he knew the kind of things she liked.

Jerry had also promised to act as nurse to the injured mosquito, Sybil, whom Freddy had brought with him from the jail. He couldn't of course serve her meals, but mosquitoes are used to going for many days without eating, and Sybil assured him that her wing would be healed long before it would be necessary for her to use it in the search for food.

Later on, the ant and the mosquito became fast friends. Sybil continued to live in her matchbox in the drawer, flying out at dusk, and again at dawn, to look for something to eat. Their experiences in life had been so different that they had a great deal to talk about, and they sometimes sat up half the night exchanging tales of their adventures. Before her wing was well enough so that Sybil could fly, she used to get exercise by climbing out of her matchbox and taking walks, first around inside the desk drawer, and then later around the pig pen, with Jerry.

Fido was rather jealous of her; he snarled whenever she came near him, and several times tried to bite her, until Jerry gave him a good licking. Then he merely growled at her and backed into a corner. Eventually he stopped that too, but they never became really good friends.

It still lacked two hours of daylight when Jinx, booted and spurred, with his sombrero on and his gun belt strapped about his middle, rode up on Bill and scratched at the pig pen door.

Freddy came out. He swung into the saddle and the two friends rode off up the slope back of the pig pen, avoiding the duck pond and the woods where their friends lived. Crossing a corner of the Witherspoon farm, Jinx began to laugh. "Wonder what Mrs. Bean will say when she comes down and smells that kitchen this morning."

"She'll think Mr. Bean has got some new tobacco that's even stronger than that stuff he usually smokes. 'Old Overshoes,' is that the name of it?"

"That's what Mrs. Bean calls it. It's 'Overton' or 'Overbridge' or something like that. That smell'll be gone after he's smoked his after-breakfast pipe."

"Maybe," said Freddy doubtfully. "What I'm wondering about is how the cannibal home folks are going to receive the army when it marches in, all perfumed up. We ought to dab a little on the queen so she'll feel at home when she gets back."

"Speaking of ants," said Jinx, "that reminds me: there was a committee of ants from one of these ant hills here this afternoon—Jerry talked to them. They've found that mole's money and stuff."

Freddy pulled up suddenly. "Samuel's treasure? Good grief, and you didn't tell him about it? We'll have to go back, Jinx, and find him— help him get the stuff into the bank vaults."

"Oh, rats!" said the cat. "It's safe where it is. And if you go back now, somebody'll see you, and you want everybody to think you're in jail."

"Can't help it," Freddy said, and reined Cy around. "We can get it done before daylight. He's been coming into the bank or up to my place five or six times a day, asking if anything has been found. Why didn't Jerry tell me?"

"I told him not to. I knew you'd want to go dig it up. But if you're seen here it'll get the sheriff in trouble, and you too. Darn it, you're a dangerous criminal, Freddy; you're not supposed to be at large."

The pig said: "I know. Well, the only fair thing is to put it up to Samuel. Come on."

The mole was living in a tunnel among the grass roots in the meadow back of the pig pen. They had arranged to signal to him by rapping three times on a big rock that stuck out of the ground near the tunnel. Jinx rapped with his pistol butt, and a few seconds later the earth beside him bulged up and the mole's snout poked out into the air.

"Yes," he said. "What's wanted? I say what's wanted?"

"You're wanted, mole," said Freddy. "Some ants have discovered your treasure. It's in the —where is it, Jinx?"

"They said there's a tunnel begins just by the east gatepost, and you go along that for two minutes, then you come to a fork and you turn left and walk for half a minute and turn right at an intersection, and thirty paces along this tunnel (that's ant paces, of course) there's a room hollowed out. It's sealed up, so you can't find it unless you know where it is. And there's the stuff."

"But hold on a minute," said Freddy. "Two minutes. That's ant walking time. How far can an ant walk in two minutes?"

"I went to an ant field-day once," said the cat, "and I remember the ant that won the five-yard dash did it in just under a minute and a half. That's about—let me see, ten feet a minute. In grass, of course."

"But that was a racing ant," said Samuel. "An ordinary ant, just walking along and looking around—well, knock off a foot, anyway. Say nine feet a minute."

"Well, now you know, anyway," said Jinx impatiently. "Dig it up and put it in the bank; the boys there'll fix you up with a safe-deposit hole. Come on, Freddy." And he swung into the saddle.

"Hey, where you going?" the mole demanded. "Aren't you going to help me get the stuff to the bank? I can't carry it alone. I say I can't carry it alone."

"We haven't time now," said Jinx. "We've got to get going before daylight."

"We're going on a riding trip," Freddy said. "We're going off to seek adventure."

"Oh, boy!" Samuel exclaimed. "I've always wanted to do that. Take me along, will you?"

They shook their heads. "Can't be done. You couldn't ride a horse if we had one for you."

"I'll give you my emerald ring if you'll take me. You could put me in a basket and tie it behind Freddy's saddle." And then, as they still shook their heads: "Gosh, a fine generous pair you turned out to be! Won't let me go on your trip, and won't even help me take my stuff over to the bank for safekeeping. O.K. then, why should I be helpful to you? Oh, I know you want me to keep quiet about your being out of jail, pig. Well, I won't keep quiet. I say I won't keep quiet. I'm going to tell everybody."

Cy was staring at the eastern sky. "Come on, Freddy," he said impatiently. "Sun'll be up soon."

But Freddy said: "No, we'll have to take him. Can't let people know I'm not still locked up. Besides, it isn't really fair to Samuel; we did promise to take the stuff into the bank."

"I won't be any trouble, Freddy, honestly I won't," said the mole earnestly.

"Pooh," said Jinx. "It's just blackmail. All that

worried you—you said so yourself—was not knowing where your stuff was. Well, now you know.
It's safe there. And we've paid the ants for find-
ing it. What more do you want us to do, for Pete's
sake?"

"Take me on this trip," said Samuel with a
grin. He looked up at the cat with his weak little
eyes. "I won't be any bother, honestly I won't,"
he said. "And I know a lot of good stories and
songs. You'll be glad to have me with you some
of the long evenings when there's nothing to do
but sit and look at one another until it's time to
go to bed."

"Yeah," said the cat crossly, "a lot of ragged
old worn-out stories will be a lot of help. And as
far as singing goes, if you so much as sound your
A—"

Bill looked around at the cat. "Oh, put a
muffler on it, Jinx. You've got to take him, so
why be a sourpuss? Ha! Not bad. Jinx the sour-
pussy-cat! But look, he's not a bad little guy.
Break down and be pleasant about it, can't you?"

Jinx shrugged his shoulders and turned away.
Bill went back to the barn and got a basket, which
was tied on behind Freddy's saddle, and then
Samuel was put in it and they started off.

Jinx looked up at Freddy with a malicious

smile. "Look at him, Bill," he said. "Doesn't he look like a fat Indian squaw with a papoose strapped on her back? Ha, Wind-in-the-Head, what's your baby's name?"

"Going to name him after you, Jinxy-boy," said the pig. "What was it that woman called you in Centerboro the other day—oo tunnin' ickle pussytat oo. Though that would really be *your* Indian name, I suppose. How about it, Chief Ickle Pussytat?"

Freddy could almost always beat Jinx at that game. The cat changed the subject. "All right, smarty. Well, come on. Get going."

The trip had been planned for more than a year. It hadn't been easy for them to agree. Freddy had argued for Cape Cod, where he could get some sea bathing. But Jinx, who although he could swim well enough, didn't enjoy the water much, voted for Canada. He wanted to visit Montreal and Quebec, where he could hear people speak French. "I want to see if they really understand each other when they make those queer sounds," he said. "Personally I think it's just double talk. I've heard it talked on the radio, but nobody can make me believe that that stuff means anything. You and I could get up, and I could say: 'Ollicky pigglebob foozle?' and you

"Ha, Wind-in-the-Head, what's your baby's name?"

could nod your head and say: 'Mealy toofer con-
despation,' and we could say we were talking
Sanskrit and everybody'd believe us. That's what
I think French folks do when there are foreigners
around. When they're alone they probably talk
as good English as we do.''

So they had decided that both Montreal and
Cape Cod were a long distance away, and it
might be better just to ride eastward on back
roads into New England. "Just sort of wander
along without trying to get anywhere specially,''
Freddy said. "It'll be more fun that way." And
Jinx had agreed.

So now they turned their mounts' heads, and
trotted eastward into the sunrise.

They had gone perhaps half a mile cross-country when Jinx, turning to look behind him, said:
"What's that?"

High in the western sky something glittered
and flashed. It stopped, and they could see
nothing, then it flashed again.

"What on earth!" said Freddy.

"I know what it is," said Cy. "It's J. J. It's the
sun reflected on his glasses."

Mr. J. J. Pomeroy, head of the A.B.I., was a
very nearsighted robin. He had once mistaken
Freddy's tail for a worm and pinched it rather

severely. As a result, and to prevent similar attacks, Freddy had taken him to an oculist and had him fitted with glasses. Now, as head of the A.B.I., he wore them on a black ribbon. He felt that this added dignity to his manner and made what he said sound more impressive.

He flew up, circled them once, then dropped down and perched on Cy's head. "I have news for you, Freddy," he said. "Bad news, I'm afraid."

Freddy said in alarm: "The Beans—has something happened to them?"

"No, no; it's Uncle Ben. He made a terrible mistake. He gave you the *good* plans. He had the good ones and the false ones in the same kind of metal cylinders, and he mixed 'em up. He let you steal the good ones. He just found out when he started work on the saucer engine that the ones he put in the bank, the ones he's working with, aren't any good. And now he wants you to bring back the other ones."

"Oh, my goodness gracious!" said the pig despairingly. "I haven't got them. I did as Uncle Ben and I decided—I let the spies steal them."

CHAPTER

13

"Darn it," said Freddy, "there goes our trip again. We'll have to get those plans back."

"Well," said Jinx, "we got farther this time. Last time we only got as far as the bank. But look, Freddy, this is a job for the F.B.I. You ought to turn it over to them."

Freddy said: "No, if Interminable Motors, who are building the saucer, find out Uncle Ben got the plans mixed up, and has been working on the wrong ones all this time, they may just refuse to go on with it. It makes him look pretty silly. The same with the F.B.I. and the Air Force. Those people don't know Uncle Ben the way we do. They'll say he's unreliable and can't be trusted, and like as not they'll lose interest in the whole thing."

"And I for one wouldn't blame 'em," put in Samuel. "Anybody who'd mix up as important plans as that, I wouldn't trust him to build a little red express wagon. I say I wouldn't trust him to go down to the store for a can of beans."

"That's why I say you don't know Uncle Ben. He isn't the kind of person you'd send for a can of beans. It's too unimportant. Unimportant things go right in one ear and out the other with him. But important things, like his atomic engine, and the saucer—well, look how he built that space ship. Even the self-filling piggy bank. His mind works on things like that, not on cans of beans. You're the one that ought to be sent to the store for beans."

"That's right," said Mr. Pomeroy, and Bill and Cy nodded approval.

But the mole wasn't satisfied. "Well, if he's so darn smart," he said, "why did he mix up the plans? And if he knows all about how the saucer works, why can't he build it right out of his head? Why does he need the plans?"

Mr. Pomeroy said: "He's talked to me about that. He knows how a saucer works all right. But to build one, he had to do a lot of very complicated mathematical work, and then put it down on paper. To get the plans so he could work at them, he'd have to do that work all over again, and it would take a year or more."

"We're wasting a lot of time here in talk," said Bill suddenly.

"That's right," said Jinx. "We know where those spies have holed up. It was lucky that the thief found Cy there when he got out of the jail window. You remember where you took him, don't you, Cy?"

"Sure. Go west on the back road between our woods and the Big Woods, past the Margarine place about two miles. 'Tisn't a farm; I guess it's more of a summer place with lots of lawn.

An old-fashioned place, with a sort of turret at one corner."

"We better go case the joint, Freddy," said Jinx. "But you can't go in that cowboy outfit— they've seen you in that."

"I know the house you mean," said Mr. Pomeroy. "The old Lenihan place. I didn't know that was where the plans had been taken, but I knew there was something queer about it, because all the spies have stopped watching the jail. They're watching that house now. My operatives have been reporting every hour, and they're all there."

"Exactly," said Freddy. "And my guess is the plans will stay there for a while. They can't be got out easily while all those other spies are watching. I agree, Jinx, that we've got to watch, too. But if we want to find out anything we've got to have a first-class disguise. We've got to fool the people outside the house as well as those inside. And somehow we've got to get inside and find the plans.

"But we can't do the job alone. I've got a scheme that I think maybe will work, but we need a lot of help. And I think we'd better call a meeting. As long as we thought the spies had the false plans, and we didn't want to get them back, it was better not to tell anybody about it.

But I'm supposed to be in jail; I don't want to be seen by anybody but just my friends who won't talk. You call the meeting for after dark tonight. I'll come up then."

"You want the flag of the F.A.R. run up?" Mr. Pomeroy asked.

The F.A.R. was the First Animal Republic, which had been formed several years ago with Mrs. Wiggins as president. Its flag, with two stars for Mr. and Mrs. Bean, and thirteen stripes for the thirteen animals who had gone on that famous trip to Florida, when hoisted over the barn, was the signal for a mass meeting.

Freddy said: "No. We don't want everybody. Not for this. Just the old crowd, and—oh, you know all the old stand-bys, Jinx. So do you, J. J. If we need more later we can draft them. But have Uncle Ben there. And the Beans, if they'll come. Mr. Bean may not want to—it makes him nervous to hear us talk. But—well, do the best you can."

"And how about me?" said Samuel, suddenly sticking his nose up over the edge of the basket. "I say how about me?"

In the shock of learning that the spies had got the correct plans for the saucer engine, Freddy had forgotten the mole. He looked hard at him.

Could this animal be trusted? Of course he had lived on the farm all his life, but he was not a citizen of the F.A.R.; indeed few of the animals had seen him, he spent so much of his time underground. But that didn't mean that he wasn't a loyal American. Anyhow, he knew too much now to be just turned away.

"Why, sure you're going to the meeting," said the pig. "And I think we can find something for you to do, too."

Samuel thanked him. "And I want to tell you, Freddy," he said, "I wouldn't have told anybody you were out of jail, even if you hadn't let me come on your riding trip. Honest I wouldn't. That was just a bluff to make you take me. I say that was just a bluff."

Freddy was pleased at this. He had felt all along that the mole was probably an honest fellow. Moles in general have a name for being reliable and straightforward in their dealings, though often cranky and irritable. So he and Cy and Samuel, when the others had left, rode back into the Big Woods and spent the rest of the day in hiding, talking over and adding improvements to Freddy's plan. And when it began to grow dark, they went down to the meeting in the barn.

Freddy's plan wasn't a very good one. It was

pretty sketchy. But as no one had a better one
to offer, it was adopted unanimously. In the Bean
barn there was an old-fashioned gypsy caravan—
sort of a small house on wheels—that Madame
Delphine, the fortune-teller with Mr. Boomschmidt's circus, had lived in for several years on
the road, until Mr. Boomschmidt had bought her
a trailer. A short distance back of the Lenihan
house there was a brook, and a little way down
the brook was a grove where gypsies sometimes
camped. Freddy's idea was that they should
disguise themselves as gypsies and camp in the
grove. None of the spies would suspect gypsies
of having any interest in the saucer plans, and
there might be an opportunity to get into the
house. In any case, they would be on the spot,
and Freddy was sure that he could think of some
way of getting the plans back.

After the meeting Freddy went up to the pig
pen and rummaged among the trunks and boxes
of old costumes that he used as disguises in his
detective work and pulled out several bright-
colored skirts which Mrs. Bean had once short-
ened for him so that he could pose as a gypsy
fortune-teller. It was a costume he had never
worn, and he was eager to see if he could get
away with it. On his head he wore a black wig

with two long black braids, and he had two brass curtain rings fastened in his ears for earrings. His false hair he tied up with a red and green scarf.

The Beans had come to the meeting, and Mrs. Bean laughed until she cried as Freddy walked back and forth across the barn floor, trying to imitate the free stride of a gypsy woman. Even Mr. Bean made the fizzing sounds in his beard which meant that he was laughing too.

" 'Tain't bad, Freddy," he said: " 'Tain't bad at all. But pigs are too light-complected to pass for gypsies. Gypsies are swarthy. Mrs. B., how about boiling up a few of those butternuts we got down cellar? That would dye him the right color. And we'll ink in a couple of good black eyebrows, too."

The butternut water was a great improvement. They tinted Uncle Ben's face and hands with it too, because he was going along to drive the caravan. He wore blue jeans and a bright-striped shirt, a colored scarf around his head and brass earrings in his ears. And on his upper lip was the long rat-tail mustache which Freddy had worn when he was disguised as Snake Peters, the western bad man. He looked quite sinister.

None of the animals who were going gypsying

got much sleep that night. It was midnight before all preparations were made, and an hour before sunrise Uncle Ben and Freddy were hitching Hank into the shafts of the caravan. Before Charles, the rooster, had come out of the henhouse to get things started on the farm with his justly celebrated crow, the gypsies were half a mile down the road. First came the caravan, with Uncle Ben and Freddy on the little driving seat up front. Inside the caravan were the four mice, Samuel, Sniffy Wilson, the skunk, and his family, Jinx, and rabbits Nos. 12, 13, 24, and 8.

There were so many rabbits on the farm that they had numbers instead of names. Rabbits as a rule are rather flighty and unreliable, but these four had been trained by Freddy as detectives, and they had helped crack some of his most puzzling cases.

Beside the caravan walked Mrs. Wiggins, Bill, Cy, and the two dogs.

Also in the caravan was a large carton containing five hundred of the cannibal-ant soldiers. Freddy had made a deal with the captain, whose name was Grisli. "I've got your queen," he said. "She's safe and well cared for, but I don't propose to bring her back to the hill unless you do certain things for me. I want you to put your-

The Gypsies were half a mile down the road.

self and five hundred of your soldiers under my command for a few days. I will not conceal from you that our mission is dangerous—I think it likely that a number of you will get squashed."

"We do not mind being squashed in the line of duty," said Grisli in his harsh voice. "But neither I nor my soldiers wish to be squashed in vain. We know that our queen was kidnapped. If you can give me assurance that Her Majesty will be returned unharmed—"

"You know me," said the pig. "I am Freddy. I give you my word." And as the ant still hesitated: "You haven't any choice, anyway," he said. "I may not need your army at all. I don't yet know exactly how I am going to use them. But if I don't use them, I will still return your queen. Well, what's your answer?"

"As you say, we have no choice," said Grisli. "We accept." He turned and gave a short order to one of the guards, who disappeared inside the gate. And presently the soldiers came marching out. With Grisli at their head they marched— *tramp, tramp, tramp, tramp, tramp, tramp, tramp*—into the box, and Freddy tied it up with string and carried it off.

The gypsies took a roundabout route to reach their camping place. They went east for a mile down the Centerboro road, then north half a mile to the back road, on which they turned west and went on through the woods and past the Margarine property till they came to the Lenihan place. They looked at the broad lawns which swept up to the house on all sides. "Golly," said Freddy, "that's going to be a tough place to break into."

Uncle Ben said: "Tough to get out of, too."

"You mean for the spies? With the plans? I don't see how they figure they can get away with it. Did you see those cars we passed a few minutes ago? My hunch is all those other spies are working together, and they've set up a road block at the only place where these men can get out. In the other direction, the road comes to a dead end half a mile on, at a deserted farmhouse. There're two men behind the stone wall across the road there, and another behind that tree. Uncle Ben, you could work out another set of plans and build your engine, months before those boys can get out of this house, much less leave the country."

Uncle Ben shook his head. "They got it figured," he said.

"I suppose they must have," Freddy said. He sighed. "I wish I was as smart as they are."

They drove on past the house. A few hundred yards farther on they turned down a rough track that led to the grove where they were going to camp. The brook widened out into a pool where it ran through the grove, and from the farther bank one could see the turret at the corner of the Lenihan house. From the near bank a path led off through the trees toward the house. Freddy thought the spies probably came down it to go swimming.

Uncle Ben unhitched Hank from the caravan and set up a tent, while Freddy started a fire and began to get breakfast. The cannibals made camp beside the water. Jinx went scouting up the path, and the rabbits and skunks and mice plunged into the underbrush to search the grove. They came back in a few minutes to report that there were no spies between the brook and the house. Jinx came back a little later. The path led to the Lenihan back gate, he said, but the only men he had seen were stationed along the road.

They were finishing breakfast and beginning to discuss plans for getting into the house, when they heard footsteps coming down the path. They looked up to see the big man with the heavy curled-up eyebrows coming toward them among the trees. He had a shotgun under his arm.

CHAPTER
14

Freddy had a pair of gloves in his pocket. The fingers were stuffed with sand. When he pulled them on over his fore-trotters they looked enough like regular hands so that nobody would know he was a pig—as long as they didn't shake hands with him. He put them on now.

As the man came toward them, Jinx, who had been sitting by the fire, jumped up and ran across in front of him. He scowled and half lifted the gun, then lowered it again. "This your cat?" he asked Uncle Ben.

Instead of replying, Uncle Ben turned to Freddy. "Eena meena hippery dick?" he asked.

"Atcha patcha dominick," Freddy said, then turned to the spy. "It is our cat," he said.

"Is bad luck—black cat," said the man. He eyed Jinx with a sort of glowering uncertainty. Then he shrugged his heavy shoulders and jerked his thumb at Uncle Ben. "These man is not speaking English?" he asked.

"He speaks only Romany—our gypsy language," Freddy said. "Oh, yes, he knows much English, but he does not like to speak it, because he does not like American people who speak it."

"He is not liking America? He is citizen?" The man looked at Uncle Ben thoughtfully.

Uncle Ben scowled at Freddy. "Atcha patcha dominatcha," he said sharply. "Tee taw tush! Uggly buggly boo!"

Freddy hung his head as if he had been reprimanded, but it was really to hide his grin as

he replied: "Ut guzoo." Then getting rid of the
grin he looked up again. "He says I talk too
much."

"Maybe so, maybe so," said the other. He
looked around, at the caravan, at the animals.
"You have permit to camping here?" he asked.

Freddy said: "We do not need a permit. We
camp here every year—a week, a month—for
many years. The sheriff knows us. You ask him
about Jasper Field—that is my husband." He
nodded toward Uncle Ben.

"Field?" The man looked puzzled. "Is gypsy
name? Is American, no?"

Uncle Ben said angrily: "Intery mintery
cutery corn!" Then, turning his back, he walked
away.

Freddy said: "He says the name is *not* American. You have made him angry. He does not like
Americans."

The man narrowed his eyes and looked specu-
latively at Uncle Ben. Then he turned back to
Freddy. "You are fortune-teller?" he asked.

"I can tell your fortune, gentleman," said the
pig. "The past, the future—if you wish to know
it. Sometimes it is not wise to ask."

The man held out his hand. "Tell me what
you see in these hand."

But Freddy shook his head. "Not today. Zelda will not tell your fortune today. The black cat has crossed your path today; it is not a good time.

"No," he said firmly, as the man persisted, "I would not see the good things, only the bad, when the black cat has warned you. Come to-morrow. Just before sundown is the best time. Zelda will tell you then."

"Very good." As the man turned to go, he scowled at Jinx, and the cat got up and trotted deliberately across in front of him again. But this time he didn't raise the gun. He said something under his breath and disappeared up the path.

"Those counting-out rhymes make good gypsy talk," Freddy said. "But there aren't enough of them. Maybe we could use hog Latin."

"Rytay ityay extnay imetay," said Uncle Ben.

"We will," said Freddy. "We must send word to the sheriff to tell him we're real gypsies. He's sure to go ask. And that was smart of you, Jinx, to run in front of him. We know now he's superstitious, and he won't try to make us move until he has had his fortune told. I was afraid he might complain about us to the state troopers, and they'd order us to leave."

"Why didn't you tell him one?" Mrs. Wiggins

asked. "You could have given him a good one."

"I can give him a better one when I know more about the inside of the house," Freddy said. "How about it, mice; want to go up and have a try at getting in?"

The four mice jumped.

"What?" said Eeny. "*Now?*"

"Walk across that lawn in broad daylight?" Quik exclaimed.

"What do you want us to do," said Eek, "charge up that hill with probably guns trained on us from every window? You're crazy, Freddy."

"Yeah," said Cousin Augustus, "what do you think we are—a bunch of lions or something? Us mice don't operate that way."

Samuel gave a comtemptuous sniff. "Far as I can see they don't operate at all. I say they don't operate at all. Want me to go, Freddy? I can get into the house and scout around. Jinx says there's a hole to get in by, next to the cellar door."

Freddy shook his head. "You aren't used to houses, Samuel. You'd get caught."

"You're too nearsighted, anyway," said Quik. "You couldn't find out anything, and they'd see you crawling around and you wouldn't even know what hit you."

"Is that so—I say is that so? Well, *you* won't

find out anything, that's a cinch. Big cowards!"

The mice all began yelling at him at once. "Who says we're cowards? At least we aren't afraid to stay on top of the ground. Come on, Freddy, we'll go—we'll go right now." And they started up the path toward the house.

Freddy said: "No. Wait a minute. You'd really better wait until night." And as he followed along, trying to persuade them, their pace gradually slowed, and presently they stopped.

"Well, maybe you're right," said Eek. "No sense getting knocked off just to show some beetle-brained mole that we're not afraid. We'll go in tonight, as you suggest, Freddy."

Samuel snickered, but Freddy shook his head at him; and just then Jinx called: "Hey! Here comes J. J. Maybe he has some news."

The robin planed down and lit on a low branch. There was no news from the farm, he said; he just came up to see what was going on. They told him of the their encounter with the big man, and then Freddy said:

"Let me take your glasses a minute, J. J."

Mr. Pomeroy lifted the loop of ribbon over his head and handed them over. They were the kind that pinch on the nose—or rather, in Mr. Pomeroy's case, the beak.

"I thought you wore spectacles," Freddy said.

"I used to," said the robin. "The kind that hook behind your ears. Only I haven't got any ears, and I was always losing them. So I got these. Mrs. Pomeroy likes them. She says it makes me look distinguished." He stuck out his chest and looked noble.

"They do give you a sort of scholarly look," said Freddy. "Come here, Samuel; I want you to try these—see if you don't see better with them on." He perched the glasses astride the mole's nose.

Samuel swung his head slowly from side to side, then looked up at Freddy and backed off. "Goodness!" he exclaimed.

As he continued to stare, Freddy said: "Well, what's the matter?"

"Is *that* what you look like!" said the mole. "I never should have believed it—never!"

"So what?" said Freddy crossly. "Is anything the matter with me?"

"No, no," said Samuel. "No, of course not. That is . . . No, nothing at all, really. It's just —maybe it's the gypsy costume. I say maybe it's the gypsy costume. You do look fat."

"Fat! Well, I'm not skinny like—like Jinx here," Freddy said. "Pigs are—well, they're more rounded, more elegantly curved, than some animals. They—"

"I'll say they are," interrupted the mole. "Why kid yourself, Freddy? You're fat. And what's the harm in that? I say what's the harm in that?"

"Well," said Freddy, "it's not very tactful to—" But at that moment the mole looked around and saw the mice.

"Good grief!" he exclaimed. "What are those dreadful little creatures? Can those be mice? Those chinless, snake-tailed, bug-shaped things? Oh, take them away. I say take them away." He snatched off the glasses and held them out to Freddy; with the other forepaw he covered his eyes. "I've seen enough. I'm glad my eyes are bad; I don't want to see any better. I like you, Freddy. But up to today you've been just a large white blur to me, and that's the way I can feel kindly toward you."

The mice had left in a huff, and were chattering angrily together down by the water. Freddy said: "I do suppose that things look queer when you see them for the first time clearly. Mr. Pomeroy here had the same experience. Didn't you, J.J.?"

"Oh, yes," said the robin. "But after a short

"Goodness!" he exclaimed.

time you get used to your friends' faces, and they
don't make you jump any more. Why even Mrs.
Pomeroy, when I first saw her through my
glasses—well, I tell her now that she really
startled me. But of course that's an exaggera-
tion. But she did look different—not at all as I
had imagined her."

"Yeah?" said Samuel. "Well, I like my friends
to look like friends, not like something I dream
about when I've eaten too many angleworms."

"I've got an extra pair home—the spectacles
that hook over your ears," said Mr. Pomeroy.
"You're welcome to them if you can use them."

"Thanks. I guess not. They wouldn't be
much use to me underground, and on top of
the ground—well, I get along all right. What's
the use of scaring myself?"

Freddy looked at Mr. Pomeroy and shrugged
his shoulders. "Is that the way you felt when
you first got glasses, J.J.?"

"I guess I did at first. I know what he means.
But flying around, you have to see clearly. You
can run into a wire and bust your beak. Or,"
he added with a smile, "you can try to pull a
friend's tail off, thinking it's an angleworm."

"Good thing it was fastened on tight," said
Freddy.

"You could have had an artificial one," the robin said. "A long one, that you could wag. You've always wanted a waggable tail."

Freddy said: "I asked Uncle Ben if he could make me one. He said he could, but he wouldn't guarantee it would stay on. I'd look pretty silly if it fell off just when I was wagging it hard to greet the sheriff or Mrs. Peppercorn or somebody."

"Sort of undignified," said Mr. Pomeroy. "Well, I must get back. By the way, I've got a report on the men who have got that road block east of the house. They talk English part of the time, and they've been keeping watch for a helicopter. I won't give you all the details, but the way I piece it out is this: these people in the house are spies—or working for foreign agents. They are part of a larger gang, which has a secret air base in Canada—somewhere in northern Ontario. There they have long-distance planes that can fly over the pole to any country in Europe. If they can get the plans up to this air base, they can fly them to their government without interference. The trick is to get them from this house to the air base without being stopped by all these other spies that are watching the house.

"These road-block guys think that they'll try to pick up the plans with a helicopter. They think it'll come at night, and they've got guns —no big stuff, just small arms—to try to shoot it down. If that fails, they have a plane of their own at the Centerboro airfield, and they'll chase the copter and try to knock it down and grab the plans." Mr. Pomeroy took his glasses in one claw and tapped the branch thoughtfully. "I don't know how the pick-up will be made," he said, "and I don't know whether the road-block people, or the other gangs of spies, can stop it. But don't you think, Freddy, that it's too big a job for us? Don't you think we ought to call in the F.B.I.?"

"We might have to, later," said Freddy. "But I don't want to yet. For two reasons. One: the only way the F.B.I. could capture these people would be to surround the house and drive 'em out with guns and tear gas. And what would the spies do? They'd burn the plans and swear they hadn't stolen them. Then Uncle Ben would be in a nice hole. Or, two: if the automobile company and the government found that Uncle Ben was so careless as to mix up the plans, they'd think he was too silly to build the engine, and they'd call the whole thing off. Let's wait a few days and see how we make out. I've got some ideas."

Freddy did indeed have some ideas, but they weren't ideas about how to get the plans back. They were ideas about poems to write, or practical jokes to play on Jinx, or how to lose a little weight without having to stop eating. But he didn't think it necessary to explain this to Mr. Pomeroy. At this stage in a detective case, he had found that he never did have a plan; but if he just kept on nosing around and stirring things up, something would happen that he could turn to his advantage.

So as soon as it got dark that evening, they went up to the back gate of the Lenihan house. There was shrubbery about the gate, and Freddy had expected that the mice could walk right up across the back lawn in the dark and get in through the holes around the cellar door. But to his surprise, there were big electric lights on all sides of the house. The whole expanse of lawn was floodlighted as bright as day. And the mice absolutely refused to walk up across all that open lawn.

"You know perfectly well, Freddy," Eek said, "that mice never walk across an open space. They go around the edges. Even at home we never go straight across the barnyard, and this is three times as far. Mice just don't operate that way."

"Sure, we know that," said Jinx with a grin. "And we know why. Because they're always scared. People talk about scaredy-cats, but what they really ought to say is scaredy-mice. Mice are scareder than anybody."

"They are not!" said Quik, and Cousin Augustus said: "We're just smaller than other animals. We have to be careful."

"Sure, and why all these lights?" said Eeny. "It's so these people can watch to see if anybody tries to get in the house. And you bet they've got guns, too."

"But good gracious, they wouldn't shoot a mouse!" Freddy said.

"How'd we know?" said Eek. "What do we know about these people? Maybe they like to eat mice. Maybe they'd like nothing better than a nice mouse stew."

Samuel came up and nudged Freddy. "These mouse people," he said, "I can take 'em up to the cellar door without being seen. Do you want to go, mice? I say do you want to go? Then follow me." And he went up to the gate and plunged suddenly into the ground. The big electric light shone directly down on the lawn, so the little ridge that went up toward the house cast no shadow. No watcher would have noticed anything. One by one the mice went into the tunnel. Freddy watched. And after a minute or so, close to the foundation of the house and next to the cellar door, he saw a small black animal come up out of the ground, and following him, four smaller gray animals. They waved their forepaws at the gate, then the mole dove back into his tunnel, and the mice vanished through a small hole beside the door.

Pretty soon Samuel came out by the gate. "Well, I got 'em there. I say I got 'em there," he said. "Though I don't know what good they'll be, they're so darned scary. As long as none of 'em got so scared they fainted, and plugged up the tunnel. What do we do next?"

CHAPTER
15

The mice explored the cellar first. They found many interesting and unusual things—one always does in cellars—but nothing that told them anything about the present occupants of the house. At some time the house had been lived in by other humans, and by mice. The two species had evidently been on good terms—as mice and men usually are, until the mice begin to get into the package goods. There were mouse nests and there were runways up through the walls to the upper stories, and as they found later, entrances for mice gnawed in corners of nearly all the rooms. It was an easy house to explore.

On the first floor there was a good kitchen and a well-stocked pantry, but the other rooms were scantily furnished except for two machine guns at the living-room and dining-room windows, and several rifles and shotguns scattered about. There were four bedrooms on the second floor, and on a table in the largest one was the cylinder containing the good plans.

"Has Uncle Ben got the other plans, the no-good ones, with him?" Eeny asked.

"I think so," said Quik. "I think he's got two sets of false plans, just in case. They're in the locker in the caravan."

"Why couldn't we go get one of 'em and push the tube up here through the tunnel, and take this one back with us?" said Eeny.

"The tunnel isn't big enough," said Cousin Augustus. "And it isn't entirely straight; if we got stuck halfway we'd be in a nice mess."

"And how could we get it down to the cellar and out of the door?" said Quik.

"Yeah, I guess you're right," Eeny said. "But couldn't we get the plans out and chew 'em up? Then the spies couldn't use 'em."

"Neither could Uncle Ben," said Eek. "It's got to be something better than that."

There were four men in the house: Penobsky, Smirnoff, the big man with the curly eyebrows, and two other short, thickset men, with broad flat faces, whose names seemed to be Franz and Ilya. It was easy for the mice to go on exploring and still keep out of their way. They patrolled the house, but their eyes were on the windows, and if the mice ran across the floor they never noticed them.

At ten, Penobsky went to bed in the big room where the plans were, and Ilya in one of the smaller rooms. Smirnoff and Franz put out the lights inside, and took up places by windows on opposite sides of the house. Evidently they kept a twenty-four-hour watch.

About midnight the telephone rang. Penobsky answered it, but he spoke in a foreign tongue.

At the end, however, he lapsed into English. "This is you, Rendell? I do not wish to speak to you. You take your orders from Paul. . . . Yes, Friday. Or if it storms, the next calm night after that. . . . Yes, we will put the lights out at ten. Good-bye."

The mice held a whispered conference under Penobsky's bed. It was perfectly safe. A mouse's whisper is much too light to be heard unless you put your ear right down next to him. But they couldn't figure out what Penobsky had meant, and the names Paul and Rendell were unknown to them. Maybe Freddy could work it out. They decided to keep watch all night and report to him in the morning.

At two, Smirnoff and Franz went to bed and the other two took up the watch. The four mice continued to prowl about. They got into Penobsky's suitcase and found a number of letters, but they were all written in some foreign language.

"I wish I'd taken up languages," said Eeny. "Do you suppose there's anything important in these letters?" Eeny was always asking questions beginning with "Do you suppose," or "I wonder if." A lot of people do that. And of course there are never any answers.

Nobody answered this question, so Eeny went

right on. "I wonder if the mice in Europe speak foreign languages," he said. He waited for comment, and when none came: "They say foreign languages are very hard to learn, so probably they don't," he said.

"So is English a hard language to learn," said Cousin Augustus with a sniff. "I wish you'd learn to talk sense in it."

Eeny got mad and went off into Smirnoff's room. The big man was sleeping on his back with his mouth open. On the table beside the bed was a glass of water and a pistol and an open box with some pills in it. "Wonder if I can make a basket," said the mouse to himself, and he giggled and picked up one of the pills in his paws and tossed it neatly into the open mouth.

"Glug!" said Smirnoff, and he sat up suddenly and glared around him, feeling of his throat.

"Score two for our side," said Eeny to himself. He had jumped down and was under the bed. He had to stay there for about ten minutes, while the big man put on the light and looked around to try to find out what had happened.

When things had quieted down and Smirnoff was asleep again—he was on his side now and his mouth was tightly closed with one hand over it —Eeny got back on the table. He thought it might be fun to shoot off the pistol. But he couldn't find the safety catch, and that was a good thing for him, because if he had pulled the trigger and the pistol had gone off, the recoil might have knocked him across the room.

He waited a while, thinking that Smirnoff might turn over on his back again and open his mouth, and he could practice shooting some more baskets. Then he thought maybe he hadn't ought to, maybe if the man swallowed too many of his pills it might make him sick. So he went on exploring the room, taking note of everything for his report to Freddy.

It took several hours for the mice to make their reports in the morning, but when they had finished, Freddy had a pretty clear picture of the inside of the house, and of the way the spies lived.

Occasionally through the day one of the spies who had set up the road block, or who were watching the house from one side or another, would saunter past on the other side of the brook. These men apparently did not look on the gypsies as rivals. It did not occur to them that wandering gypsies, who owe allegiance to no government, would be interested in the saucer plans. But like everybody else, they were curious about gypsies, and in telling fortunes; and seeing

what they thought was a swarthy, gaudily dressed
gypsy woman, more than half of them crossed
the brook on stepping stones at the head of the
pool and asked to have their fortunes told.

It always seemed to Freddy's friends that in
even the most elaborate of his disguises, his nose
should have given him away. It was not a human
nose, it was a pig's nose. But Freddy in disguise
was like those puzzle pictures that are captioned:
"What is wrong with this picture?" You have to
hunt for the detail that is wrong. And there was
no caption under Freddy. You saw a gypsy
woman—the swarthy complexion, the black
braids, the head tied in a bright scarf, the big
earrings, the full, gaudy skirts. People see what
they expect to see. You never noticed the pig's
nose.

Freddy took in more than fifteen dollars that
day. And I think they got their money's worth.
He sat at a card table and the men laid their
hands, palms up, on the table in front of him.
He did not touch the hands but kept his sand-
filled gloves folded in his lap as he bent over to
read the lines. And he told them of success and
great obstacles surmounted, of riches, and of
hidden talents, revealed by these lines, but un-
suspected by their possessors. Every man whose

fortune Freddy told was destined to find fame and fortune as a musician, a statesman, an actor, a scientist—always in some profession which the man knew nothing about. For, as Freddy knew, it is easier to believe in a hidden talent if it is in a field of which you know nothing. And each one went away happy in the belief that he had only to give up spying and take up some other profession, to become a tremendous success.

But when Smirnoff came down the path to have his fortune told, Freddy changed his tactics. The big man pretended that the fortune-telling was just a joke, that he had come just for entertainment and to pass the time. "Is mooch money in these hand, no?" he said with a grin. "You see maybe rich wife I shall marry, eh?" But Freddy knew that he was superstitious, and could perhaps be made to believe that the gypsies could help get the plans out of the country.

"There is not much money in this hand, no," Freddy said. "There is some sickness. Not bad sickness, but you must take medicine, pills." He shook his head. "But that is not important. There is trouble—an accident. It has not happened yet. It is . . ." He paused. "Let me see if I can get it this way," he said, and closed his eyes and covered them with one of the sand-stuffed gloves.

For a minute or two he didn't say anything. Then: "I see a room," he muttered. "It has two windows to the south and two to the east, one of them cracked. The wallpaper is dark green, and there is a bright-colored calendar between the east windows. It is a picture of a little girl hugging a big dog. There is a big bed of dark wood and there is a small man in it. There is a table in the center of the room and on it is something—a sort of tube. It has something in it—could it be maps?"

At this Smirnoff, who had become more and more agitated as Freddy went on with the description of Penobsky's room which the mice had given him, drew in his breath sharply. "Stop!" he said. "How are you knowing this? You could not—"

"Quiet," said Freddy. "I see other things, too. I see a man—someone you are expecting. His name is Cran-Crandall. Wendell. I cannot make out. It is to him the accident happens. He cannot come to you. There are men—they are shooting at him." Freddy stopped suddenly and uncovered his eyes. "That is all I can tell you, gentleman," he said.

"Let me see if I can get it this way," and closed his eyes.

Smirnoff stared at him. It was plain that he was thinking that there was no way in which this gypsy could have known about Penobsky's room, about the tube containing plans on the table, or that someone named Rendell was coming. After a moment he said: "This man you call Crandall —you are saying he cannot come here?"

Freddy sat up straight. "That is your fortune, my gentleman. That is all I can tell you." Then, as the spy merely continued to stare at him, he said: "That is what I have seen with the eyes of the mind. But with these eyes"—he touched them—"I have seen other things. Men behind trees and walls, watching the house. Men down the road and up the road, armed men. What will you give Zelda if she can drive them away? So that the road is open?"

Smirnoff narrowed his eyes and stared at Freddy. After a minute he said: "The road—is not need to be open. But you can do thees—drive these men?"

"For one hundred dollars, yes."

The spy didn't haggle. When the road was clear and there were no more men lurking behind trees and walls, he would pay Freddy the hundred dollars.

The next morning Freddy took one of the

tubes containing false plans and strapped it to his leg under his skirts. He saddled Cy and rode slowly down to where the spies had their road block. There were a dozen cars parked beside the road, and back among the trees were a number of tents. Men came out of them as Freddy rode up, and pushed up around him, asking to have their fortunes told.

"Yes, I will tell them," he said. "But one at a time. And not with you all crowding around. That tent there." He pointed. "Is there a table there? Good. I will go there."

So he dismounted and went into the tent and sat down at the table. The first man was short and slant eyed; Freddy thought him some kind of an Oriental. The others came up close to the door to listen, but Freddy shooed them away. Then when nobody could hear what he said:

"Listen," he muttered. "I have the flying saucer plans. Do you want to buy them?"

"*You* have them?" the man exclaimed.

Freddy reached under his skirt and pulled out the tube. He took the cap off and pulled the roll of plans part way out and let the man assure himself that they were what he said they were.

"How did you get these?" the man demanded.

"I have known this house many years," said

Freddy. "There is a secret entrance. But what does that matter to you? Do you want them?"

"How much you want for them?" the other asked.

Freddy knew that such plans, if they were good, would be worth millions. He didn't want to take money for false ones, even from an enemy of his country. But to hand them over for nothing, or for a small fraction of their value, would make the spies suspicious.

He shook his head. "Make me an offer," he said.

The man said: "I must consult my associate." He went to the door of the tent, and beckoned. Another slant-eyed man who might have been his brother came into the tent. They talked in a language which Freddy couldn't even put a name to. It didn't look like a consultation to Freddy; it sounded more as if the first man was giving orders to his associate. And after a minute the latter went away.

"We will pay generously for these plans," said the first man, coming back to the table. "But you must understand that we do not have a large sum of money with us. We will have to arrange —" He broke off, as a car starter whined briefly and then merged into the roar of a racing engine. He hesitated a moment, then suddenly grabbed up the tube and shoved the table hard into Freddy, so that the pig went over backwards in his chair. And he dashed out of the tent.

Freddy picked himself up, shook out his skirts, and ran after him. The second slant-eyed man was at the wheel of a big car which was already in motion. The first man, with the tube in plain sight under one arm, was running beside the car, holding to the door handle. As he scrambled in, Freddy began to yell. "Stop him!" he shouted. "He's stolen the plans! He's got the plans of the flying saucer!"

All the men who were waiting to have their fortunes told suddenly ran for their cars. Two men with walkie-talkies were shouting excitedly into them, and other men, having seen that something was going on, from where they were watching, up the road or out in the fields, suddenly appeared and were dashing for their cars and motorcycles, which had been parked wherever there was a little cover behind walls and among bushes and trees. In two minutes they were converging on the road, down which rushed the stream of cars in pursuit of the thieves. In five minutes the landscape, which had been alive with running figures, was empty of men, and the roar of the speeding cars died away to the east. Freddy called to Cy, hopped into the saddle, and went back to the camp.

CHAPTER
16

Freddy found Mr. Pomeroy waiting for him when he got back to the camp.

"I've found out who that fellow is that the mice heard the spies talk to over the phone," said the robin. "Fellow named Rendell, remember?

Well, he's got a helicopter down at the fair-grounds, and he takes people up for five dollars a ride. He must be the man I heard those road-block guys talking about. The one that's sup-posed to pick up the plans and take 'em up to the secret base in Canada."

"That's right," said Freddy. "And it'll be a cinch, now that the road block is cleared up and all the other spies are gone. I guess maybe I wasn't so smart to get rid of them. There'll be nobody to shoot him down. All he's got to do is come down on the lawn and they'll give him the tube."

"I don't believe he plans to land," said Mr. Pomeroy. "He's got a basket on a long rope—I looked the copter over this morning. He'll hover, and let down the basket for them to put the tube in. And according to what the mice heard he's to come Friday, or the next calm night if Friday's stormy. Today's Thursday. I wonder why they put it off so long."

"Waiting for the dark of the moon," said Freddy.

"Oh, sure. But golly, Freddy, we've got to do something quick. If he gets away with the plans— Psst! Here come the spies!" he whispered, and flew up into one of the trees.

Penobsky and Smirnoff were coming down the path from the house. They seemed to be unarmed. They stopped in front of Freddy, and Penobsky said: "My associate tells me that he promised you a hundred dollars if you could drive away all these people who have been watching us. You seem to have done it. We will pay you. But we must first be sure that they do not come back. If they are not back by Saturday morning, we will pay you then."

"That was not the agreement," Freddy said. "I have driven them away. I want the money." He didn't want to take money from the spies at all, but he thought he ought to protest.

Penobsky smiled and shook his head. "It is no good to us if they come back," he said.

Freddy wondered where Uncle Ben was. An hour or so ago he had gone up the brook with a fishing rod, to find out if any spies were still watching the house. If he would only come back, with his shotgun, there would be a good chance of capturing these two. Then there would be only the two others to deal with. Just how he would deal with them he didn't know, but Penobsky and Smirnoff, as prisoners, would be something to bargain with. But he'd frighten them off if he called Uncle Ben.

Freddy's back was to the caravan, about which stood Mrs. Wiggins, Bill, and the two horses. The dogs were pretending to be asleep under the wagon, and Jinx was sitting beside them. Freddy motioned to them, behind his back, to come closer. Then with a quick jerk he pulled the black wig and the bright scarf from his head and tossed them to the ground. "Remember me?" he said.

"Hey!" Penobsky exclaimed. "You were in the jail. You're that educated pig of Bean's that stole the flying saucer plans!"

"And you're the one that stole them from me," said Freddy.

"That's right." Penobsky grinned at him. He didn't seem at all alarmed.

"Ha!" said Smirnoff. "This is clever piggy you are telling me about it. He does sleeping walk, eh?" He winked good-naturedly at Freddy.

But Freddy said sharply: "Put your hands up!" and he pulled the cap pistol from the pocket of his skirt and pointed it at them.

It was one of those cap pistols that you load with a coiled ribbon of caps, so that it shoots a cap as often as you pull the trigger until the coil is used up. The two spies laughed heartily and held their hands above their heads. "Sure, sure," said Penobsky. "We mustn't take chances with such a dangerous gunman."

Smirnoff pretended to be frightened. "You no shoot poor old Smirnoff, Mr. Piggy, eh?" He made his knees shake.

But Freddy was serious. "This is not a toy, gentlemen," he said. "This is an atomic pistol, invented by Mr. Benjamin Bean. It is the Benjamin Bean Practical Disintegrator. You see that bird up there?" He pointed to where Mr. Pomeroy perched on a twig some ten yards distant. "Watch him. You will see him fall." He spoke more loudly than usual, so that the robin would know what was expected of him. Then he pointed the pistol and pulled the trigger.

The cap snapped, and Mr. Pomeroy, grabbing at his glasses with one claw, tumbled off the twig. He fell straight down for ten feet, then spread his wings and planed off into the field across the brook.

The spies stopped laughing abruptly. They knew that Freddy was associated with Uncle Ben. They knew Uncle Ben's reputation. Freddy could see what they were thinking—that a man who could build a flying saucer could perfectly well build a practical disintegrator. And after all, the bird *had* been knocked from the tree.

Penobsky pulled himself together. He tried to laugh. "Phooey," he said. "The bird flew away." His hands came down.

"Keep your hands away from your pockets," Freddy ordered, and swung the pistol from one to the other. "You still are unconvinced? Then watch that cat." He pointed the pistol at Jinx and pulled the trigger.

The cat yowled, jumped in the air, rolled over twice and came to rest on his back, all four legs in the air, even his tail sticking straight up.

"The darn clown!" Freddy said angrily to himself. "Doesn't he realize that this business is serious? I wish he wouldn't always try to be funny."

Smirnoff went over to Jinx, prodded him, rolled him over. The cat was limp. He picked him up by the tail and tossed him over toward the caravan. Jinx fell in a heap and didn't stir. Freddy thought: "I take it all back—that was a good performance. My gosh, I believe we've put it over!"

The spies looked at each other. There was doubt in their eyes. Penobsky's hand moved toward his coat pocket, but Freddy swung the cap pistol toward him, and the movement stopped. Smirnoff glanced over his shoulder

toward the path and gave a startled exclamation.
His retreat was cut off; Mrs. Wiggins had moved
up silently behind him; the tip of her left horn
was three inches from his coat tails. The goat and
the horses and the dogs were moving in too.

"Look here, what *is* all this?" Penobsky exclaimed. "We haven't got those plans. They've
been passed on long before this."

Freddy said: "No. They are in the house.
You, Mr. Penobsky, are my prisoner. Mr. Smirnoff is free to go. When he brings the plans to us,
we will release you. If he does not return with
them, we will inform the F.B.I. and turn you
over to them."

Penobsky shrugged his shoulders. "You seem
to have the advantage of us," he said dejectedly.
He said something to his associate in a strange
language. The other answered shortly. "I have
told Smirnoff to get the plans," Penobsky said.

Smirnoff turned as if to push Mrs. Wiggins
aside and go up the path to the house, and it was
in just those few seconds when the two men were
separated and Freddy could no longer threaten
both with the cap pistol, that disaster overtook
him. Smirnoff swung around, and there was a
heavy pistol in his fist, and at the same moment
Penobsky struck down hard on Freddy's fore-

trotter. The cap pistol spun out of his grasp. Penobsky dove for it, pointed it at Freddy and pulled the trigger.

Freddy had only a split second in which to choose what to do. But it took him less than that to realize that the only sensible thing now was to play dead. He gave a squeal and two groans and fell flat on his face. It was a good fall, he thought; almost as good as Jinx's.

The animals had dropped back at the sight of Smirnoff's gun. The spies stood over Freddy, talking. Penobsky knelt down and felt of the pig's left fore-trotter. The left one still had the sand-filled glove on; Freddy had taken off the right glove so that he could handle the cap pistol. It apparently didn't occur to Penobsky, as he felt the cold glove and tried to find the pulse, that he must be feeling of a fake hand, since pigs aren't usually equipped with hands and feet. He looked up at Smirnoff and shook his head as much as to say: "I guess he's gone." They talked for a minute, then Penobsky looked Freddy over for a bullet hole. Freddy held his breath.

After a few minutes Penobsky got up. The two men examined the cap pistol, shaking their heads incredulously. Smirnoff handed his gun to Penobsky and took the pistol. He pointed it at

Bill, who had wandered off toward the water, and pulled the trigger.

Bill was quite willing to oblige. He felt that he could put on a better show than Jinx had. He reared up on his hind legs, turned two cartwheels, and then tried a back somersault. It was perhaps fortunate that he slipped, for the spies would certainly be suspicious if he had succeeded with such complicated acrobatics. He fell and bumped his head on a rock. But he had the sense to lie still.

The men walked over and inspected him; then they looked at the pistol again, and shook their heads over it. But evidently they were now convinced that it was all that Freddy claimed for it. They went back to Freddy, talked for a time, then Smirnoff pocketed the cap pistol, heaved the pig up on his shoulder, and started up the path with him.

At the house, Penobsky opened the cellar door, and Smirnoff carried Freddy down and dumped him on the concrete floor. Then he went back and got Bill and Jinx. Evidently they did not realize that the other animals could talk, and hoped to conceal from Uncle Ben that their three companions had been shot.

When the men had gone, Freddy said in a

whisper: "You all right, Bill? You took a pretty hard fall."

"My left horn aches," said the goat. "It was a neat performance though, wasn't it?"

"Neat like falling downstairs," said Freddy.

"Pity you didn't break your neck," said Jinx. "That would have made it perfect."

"Aw, you're just jealous," said Bill. "Look, Freddy, what do we do next? Neither door is locked, the one to the outside nor the one to the kitchen. Could we get the plans?"

"I think so," said Freddy. "You see that electric meter over there on the wall, and the big switch by it? If we wait till night, and pull that switch, I bet it will cut off all the lights, both outside and inside the house. Then if you two get up into the house and make a racket and draw the men off from Penobsky's room, I can grab the plans and run."

"Where to?" Jinx asked.

"That's a good question. Not to the caravan. Uncle Ben will have to hitch up Hank and drive off. He'd better saddle Cy and leave him down at the end of the path. He can't saddle Bill; you'll have to ride him bareback, Jinx, till we catch up with the caravan. Uncle Ben can pull off the road and wait for us in the Big Woods."

"Pity you didn't break your neck," said Jinx.

A small hoarse voice said: "Uncle Ben has come back and he's pulling out. I say he's pulling out. He thinks they've spotted who he is."

"Hello, Samuel," said Freddy. "Where are the mice?"

"He's taken them along, and the rabbits and the skunks. He got those ants to get back in the carton, too, and took them. He said you wanted them."

"That's right," Freddy said. He told the mole what they planned to do, and then he said: "You'd better go back and tell Uncle Ben to saddle Cy and leave him, and then get aboard the caravan yourself. You don't want to be left behind."

So Samuel went back through the hole and down the tunnel, and the three victims of the Benjamin Bean Practical Disintegrator settled down to wait for it to get dark.

It was a long wait. They didn't dare talk much, and only Jinx, who moved silently, could do much exploring. But at last they heard a clock upstairs strike eleven. Two of the men, they knew, would be in bed and probably asleep, the other two would be on guard at the kitchen and parlor windows. Freddy got up. "All right, boys," he said. "Now you know what we have to do."

They crept up the stairs. The cellar door fortunately didn't open directly into the kitchen, but into a sort of vestibule between kitchen and dining-room. Very cautiously Freddy opened it a crack, and Jinx crept through. There were no lights on inside the house, but there was a good deal of illumination that came through the windows from the floodlights outside. The cat came back in a minute or two to report that Penobsky was on watch at the parlor window and Franz at the kitchen window. Penobsky's bedroom then was empty, and the tube of plans was on the table.

"O.K.," said Freddy. "Let's go." He went through the dining-room to the front hall, and tiptoed up the stairs. As he reached the top, all the lights suddenly went off. Bill had pulled the switch. At the same moment there was a series of appalling crashes from the dining-room. Jinx was creating a diversion.

Cats seldom break dishes. They pride themselves on being able to leap from the floor to a mantelpiece crowded with bric-a-brac and thread their way from one end to the other without even brushing against the most fragile and delicately balanced vase. It is a dangerous sport—for Jinx, a broken knickknack meant a licking and no cream for a week. Now, however, he was trying to break everything he could, and he found that it was lots more fun than being careful. He knocked a big bowl off the dining-room table, then jumped to the mantel where he pushed off two pitchers and some glass candlesticks and a big clock, which made a most satisfying smash when it hit the marble hearth. He heard thumps and footsteps upstairs, but before they came down he had time to leap to the sideboard and sweep off a whole row of fancy plates, topping off with a big glass punch bowl. A flashlight flickered in the hall now, and he jumped down and stood close beside the hall door. As two men came pounding into the room, he slipped out without being seen and went back down cellar.

Freddy had ducked into Penobsky's room when Smirnoff and Ilya came out of their rooms and hurried downstairs. The tube was on the table. He grabbed it, but at the head of the stairs he hesitated. Flashlights were busy in the lower hall, and he heard someone going down the cellar stairs to see what had happened to the lights. He turned back into the room and tried first one window and then the other. But he couldn't raise either one. He sneaked across the hall into one of the back rooms. As he struggled with the window the floodlights outside suddenly went on. He saw Bill and Jinx racing down the path from the back door to the gate. The window went up. He climbed up on the sill with the tube in his mouth; it was his only chance; the drop, he was sure, wouldn't hurt him much.

And then a voice behind him said: "Hold it!" and the light in the room went on. Ilya stood there, a huge man in red-and-white-striped pajamas, covering Freddy with a gun.

The gun looked at Freddy with its big black eye, and Freddy looked back at it for a moment in silence. Then he climbed down from the window sill and handed the tube to the spy.

CHAPTER
17

Half an hour later Freddy was back in the cellar, but this time he was tied up tightly with clothesline. They hadn't treated him too badly. They put him on an old mattress, and Penobsky assured him that they wouldn't shoot him.

"There'd be no point in it," he said. "All we want is to get the saucer plans away from here without trouble. After that we will have no further interest in you. We'll let you go. We'll even give you back your pistol."

"Ah, those disindegrinder?" said Smirnoff. "Was smart idea. How you train those animals they should play dead like that, eh?" He whacked Freddy good-naturedly on the shoulder.

Freddy was not deceived by their apparent friendliness, however. He knew that either of the spies would shoot him without thinking about it twice if it would be the slightest help to them. If they shot him now he would be much more bother to them than if they kept him prisoner and let him go later. There wasn't a thing he could do.

As soon as they had gone upstairs he tried to work the ropes loose. But though he twisted and strained at them, the knots held. In adventure stories that he had read, the hero, when he was tied up, always found something sharp, a broken bottle or a bit of tin, that he could rub the ropes on until they frayed and parted. But though he rolled all over the cellar, Freddy couldn't find a thing. At last, tired out, he rolled back on to the mattress and fell into an uneasy sleep.

When he woke again the floodlights were still on outside, but far away he heard a rooster crow, so he knew that it must be nearly morning. The rooster crowed again, and he thought that back in the Bean farmyard Charles would just be coming sleepily out of the henhouse to fly up on the fence and start the day. He was pretty uncomfortable. You try sleeping all night with your hands tied behind you and you will see why. To pass the time he thought he'd try to make up a poem.

"O calm indeed is the prisoner pig,
  Remarkably calm is he,
He's as merry and gay as the well-known grig—
  (Whatever a grig may be.)
On the cold stone floor of his dungeon cell,
He does not sob and he does not yell;
To see him you'd think he was feeling swell,
  As he smiles so gallantly.

"But pigs are brave, and pigs are bold,
  With nerves as strong as steel.
When wounded in battle, so I'm told,
  They never squeak or squeal.
They know no fear and they know no dread;
And where lions and tigers fear to tread

They rush right in. When they growl, it's said,
    Even elephants reel."

Freddy repeated this aloud to himself, nodding his head with satisfaction. And a small voice said: "You've 'been told,' eh? And you've 'heard it said.' That's hearsay, Freddy; that's not evidence."

Another voice said: "And I'll bet that where you heard it said, was right inside your foolish head."

"Give us the old growl, Freddy," said a third voice.

"Hey, mice," said Freddy, rolling over so that he could look toward the door, "how did you get back here? I thought you went with Uncle Ben in the caravan."

"Sure," said Eeny. "We were all waiting just at the edge of the Big Woods. We heard Cy coming, and we thought you'd be riding him. But you weren't, and he told us that they'd caught you. So we came back. Come on, boys, get at those ropes."

The mice swarmed over him, gnawing at the clothesline. Samuel was with them, but he did little work. He sat on Freddy's chest, lecturing him on the folly of his arrangements for getting the plans. Freddy should have done this and he should have done that. "You ought to have sneaked up and got the plans and taken them down cellar before you pulled that switch," he said. "You ought not to have turned Jinx loose in the dining-room till you were ready to go out the cellar door. You ought to—"

"Oh, shut up, Samuel," Cousin Augustus interrupted. "You're so smart, why didn't you go up and get the plans yourself?"

"Well, I'd have done a better job. I say I'd have done a better job. We wouldn't have had to risk all our lives coming back here again."

"Golly," said Eek, "these ropes sure are dry. Why don't you go up in the kitchen, Samuel, and see if you can't find some bacon fat to rub on 'em. Make 'em taste better."

"I wouldn't do this for anybody but you, Freddy," said Quik. "Sets my teeth on edge."

Pretty soon the ropes parted and Freddy sat up and shook himself. "Well, I'm certainly grateful to you boys for coming back," he said. "I don't think these people were going to shoot me —that would be foolish, because once the plans are taken away from here and on their way to some foreign country, I can't do them any harm, and they'll just disappear."

"Yeah," said Eeny, "and maybe they wouldn't even bother to turn you loose. You could have stayed here till you dried up and blew away."

"That's true," said Freddy. "But besides that, you may have done a big service to your country by coming back. Now maybe we can get the plans back for Uncle Ben."

"You mean you're going to try the same stunt again tonight?" Eek asked.

"No. I've got a better idea. You remember that Rendell? Tonight's Friday night; that's when he's supposed to come. I've got to go down to the fairgrounds and see him. As soon as it gets dark I'll make a break. You'd all better go out now and have Cy take you down to where the caravan's waiting in the Big Woods. Then have him come back and wait at the end of the path. And tell Uncle Ben to stay in the woods till I get there."

The mice were curious to know what Freddy intended to do, but he refused to discuss it. "You go on," he said. "I've got a lot of thinking to do between now and dark. Go on; don't bother me." So they arranged the ropes to look as if Freddy was still tied up, and then they went.

It was a long day for Freddy with nothing to eat or drink. Nobody came down cellar, and the only people there were a couple of spiders who wouldn't have anything to do with him. They evidently thought he was a Communist, and they wouldn't talk to him but just sat up in their web and sneered at him. He tried to compose a few poems, but in spite of all the stories about poets writing masterpieces while starving in attics, he found that he couldn't even string two rhymes together on an empty stomach. "Of course I'm not in an attic, anyway," he said to himself. "I'm in a cellar. But I don't see why that should make any difference." And then he tried to make a rhyme out of that.

> *"A poetic young feller*
> *Once lived in a cellar.*
> *'Twas damp and rheumatic*
> *So he moved to the attic,*
> *Where the verses he scribbled*
> *Were really much sweller*
> *Than the rather too ribald*
> *Ones done in the cellar."*

He had to repeat this out loud to see how it sounded, and of course the spiders heard it. One of them looked at the other and raised his eyebrows and said: "Really!" And the other just sniffed.

This irritated Freddy. "I wasn't addressing you," he said, "and I wasn't asking for your comments."

"I don't see that there are really any comments that we would care to make," said one spider. And the other said: "Unfortunate that there is no attic in this house."

No one would blame Freddy if he had gone over and squashed both those spiders. Like most poets, he was enraged to have even his weaker efforts criticized. But he controlled himself. "I don't know what you expect," he said. "You can't make verses when you're suffering from hunger and thirst."

"My dear fellow," said the first spider, "we didn't expect anything." He paused a moment. "Not anything," he repeated.

Freddy turned his back and tried to take a nap.

The day came to an end at last. Freddy didn't wait until dark. He was afraid that if he did, it would be too late for what he had to do. He would just have to take a chance at being shot at when he ran out the cellar door. And that is what he did. As soon as the sun began to go down and the cellar windows to darken, he got up and pulled the switch so that the floodlights couldn't be turned on, and then he hurried up the stairs, flung open the door, and ran for his life down the path to the back gate.

There was a startled shout from the back window, but no shots followed. Out the gate he tore and into Cy's saddle; and then he was galloping off down the road toward the Big Woods.

The caravan was waiting by the side of the road. Freddy stopped only long enough to get from Uncle Ben the carton of ants, and the tube containing the second set of false plans; then with Jinx, mounted on the goat, beside him, galloped on toward Centerboro. In front of him on the saddle rested the carton containing the cannibal ants.

The fairgrounds were dark, and they pulled up just inside the gate and listened. Somewhere, at the far end away from the grandstand, an engine was ticking over quietly. It didn't sound like a car.

"That's our man," said Freddy. "Keep back out of sight. I don't think he'll dare call the police. If it comes out what he's trying to do tonight, he'll be tried for treason."

"You want me to wait here until you come back?" Jinx asked.

"Yes, you and Bill and Cy. If I have luck, I'll

be back before midnight. All right, Cy." He reined the horse forward.

There were thick woods at the far end of the fairgrounds. Just before reaching them Freddy saw the helicopter. There were no lights on the machine, but the sky was still bright enough so that Freddy could see the outline of it, and the movement of the propeller against the sky. He rode up closer, until he could make out the figure of the man at the controls.

"Mr. Rendell?" he called.

The man leaned out. "Sorry," he said. "I never take anybody up at night."

"I don't want to go up," Freddy said. "Mr. Penobsky sent me here. He wants you to take this box with you tonight, along with what you are to pick up at his place."

"Penobsky?" said Rendell. "I don't know any Penobsky. You've got the wrong man, mister."

Freddy dismounted and came up to the machine. He shoved the carton quickly in on the floor next to Rendell's seat. "Penobsky didn't have time to get in touch with you through Paul," he said, "or to try to get a message to you. He told me to come straight here. Look, I know what your job is, and what that basket's for," he said, pointing to the one with a cord attached on the seat beside the pilot. "They're waiting for you now. They weren't sure when you'd start; Penobsky was afraid he'd miss you if he came himself."

Rendell still hesitated, and Freddy decided that he'd better act at once. He reached in and lifted the cover of the carton. "O.K., Grisli," he said. "This is the guy I want worked over. Let your boys go to work."

The cannibal ants boiled up out of the box. Before Rendell could say any more they were in his hair and on his wrists and ankles, they were up his pant legs and coat sleeves, and walking down inside his collar. And they went right to work biting. Rendell gave a couple of yelps, his arms and legs jerked frantically, and then he was out of the helicopter, apparently doing some sort of a gymnastic dance that included rolling about and tearing off his clothes, as well as yelling at the top of his lungs.

Freddy clambered quickly into the seat. "All right, Grisli," he called. "Good work. You can let the guy go now. Drop off the machine, all you soldiers, and rally on the carton. I'll pick you up later. Take orders from Jinx." He tossed the carton to the ground, and taking hold of the controls, sent the helicopter straight up in the air.

Freddy had had a pilot's license for two years, but a helicopter is harder to fly than other planes, and he had had only a few hours' experience in the air in one. But Uncle Ben had given him careful instructions, and so he did not have too much difficulty making the machine go where he wanted it to. Out in the open it was still not entirely dark. It was not yet ten o'clock either —the hour at which Penobsky had said he would put out the floodlights, so that Rendell could pick up the plans without being seen. Freddy took a few turns around the fairgrounds to get the feel of the controls, and then he practiced hovering. Fortunately it was a still night; he was able to stop, hover, and drop the basket within a foot of where he wanted it nearly every time.

He waited a while after he had heard the town clock strike ten, then he started for Penobsky's. Everything went as he had planned. The house was dark, but as he flew over it, someone came down off the porch and waved a flashlight. Freddy circled round and hovered and let down the basket. When he drew it up the tube of plans was in it.

Now came the tricky part. Quickly he substituted the false plans for the real ones, then he dropped basket and rope, pretending to snatch at them and miss them as they fell at the feet of the man, who he saw was Penobsky.

The spy picked them up. "Come down, you clumsy fool!" he shouted. He held up the basket. "Come down and get it." At the same moment he turned the beam of the flashlight momentarily on Freddy.

"Hey! It's you!" he shouted. He dropped the basket and tugged a pistol out from under his coat. And Freddy opened the throttle so that the helicopter shot up and away. A couple of bullets ripped past his head, and then the house was far below and behind him, and he grinned happily. He had got back the real plans, and at the same time he had convinced Penobsky that *he* had them. There would be no more trouble for Uncle Ben. He'd be free to build his engine without being bothered.

Back at the fairgrounds Cy came trotting out to meet the helicopter. "Jinx is rounding up ants," he said. "They sure got spilled over a lot of territory when that guy went into his dance."

"Did many of 'em get squashed?" Freddy asked.

"Not many. They're pretty tough. There are

A couple of bullets ripped past his head.

some busted legs and sprained feelers, but they don't seem to mind those any more than you or I would mind a stubbed toe."

A minute later Jinx came up on Bill, and handed the carton to Freddy. He saluted. "All present or accounted for, sir," he said.

"Where's Rendell?" Freddy asked.

"After the ants got off him he ran off yelling," Jinx said.

So they left the helicopter and rode back home.

When they reached the barnyard the caravan was standing by the barn. Nobody was around, but there was a light in Uncle Ben's workshop.

"Look, Jinx," said Freddy, "the plans are safe now, but we still can't tell anybody. Until the saucer is built, I'll have to keep out of sight. I'm still supposed to be in jail. Now's the chance for us to take that trip. Let's start right now. I'll take the plans up to Uncle Ben, and you take this carton and go get the cannibal queen and take them back to the ant hill. Then get your saddlebags and meet me at the pig pen in fifteen minutes."

He dismounted and ran up the stairs to the loft and plunked the tube down on the bench in front of Uncle Ben. The old man looked up without saying anything. Then he uncapped the tube, pulled out the roll of plans, and looked them over carefully.

"Good!" he exclaimed suddenly. He beamed at Freddy, put an arm across his shoulders and clapped him on the back. Then he spread out the plans on the bench, put weights on the corners, and began to study them. He seemed to have forgotten Freddy immediately.

Uncle Ben certainly never overpraised anybody, Freddy thought. And yet he was entirely satisfied. Uncle Ben's "Good!" meant more to him than, from another man, a long oration, with flag waving and fireworks. He smiled happily as he went back down the stairs.

At the pig pen he got into his cowboy costume, and with his guitar slung over his shoulder, came out and swung into the saddle. He hadn't lit a light, and had moved very quietly, but as he sat waiting for Jinx, a small hoarse voice down near the ground said: "Hey! You promised to take me. I say you promised to take me."

"Oh, for gosh sakes!" said Cy disgustedly. "It's that Samuel Jackson again."

Freddy said: "Yeah." And then he said: "We did promise to take him, Cy."

Cy didn't say anything, but he shrugged his

shoulders so violently that Freddy's hat fell over his eyes.

Freddy said: "Look, Samuel, instead of taking you on a long hard trip, wouldn't you rather we went down right now and dug up your valuables, and put them in the bank where they'll be safe?"

"No," said the mole.

But after a minute, as nobody said anything, he said: "Yes, I'll settle for that. If you remember how to find the things. But I bet you don't —I say I bet you don't."

"Why, let's see. No, I don't believe I do. But Jinx will know. The ants that found the stuff told Jerry Peters, and Jerry told Jinx. Don't you remember? Jinx gave you very careful directions. I remember hearing him."

"Sure. Only you wouldn't go then, and now I've forgotten them."

"Well, here comes Jinx now," said Freddy, and as the cat came trotting up astride Bill, he explained the situation to him.

"Why, sure, I remember," said Jinx. "There's a hole by the east gatepost, and you go along that tunnel for two minutes, and then you come to a fork, and you turn right—no, I guess you turn left, and then you—lemme see, now; you take the left fork—no, I guess it's the right one, after all. And then you—no, no . . . oh, I don't know, I can't remember. Let's ask Jerry; he's the one that told me."

So they went into the pig pen and opened the desk drawer, and asked Jerry. And Jerry couldn't remember either. "Though there's something in it about 'twenty paces farther on.' But I don't remember farther on from what. We'll have to ask those ants. Only—well, golly, I don't remember which hill they came from."

"You see?" said Samuel triumphantly. "I knew you wouldn't remember. I say I knew you wouldn't remember. You'll have to take me."

"All right," Freddy said. "But you'll have to ride in one side of these saddlebags. The basket's no good—you'd bounce right out when Cy started to trot."

So they set out, up the slope from the barnyard, and leaving the Big Woods on the left, on toward Otesaraga Lake. At the top of the hill overlooking the next valley they turned and looked back. Nothing could be seen of the farm, but from out of the blackness where it lay, a little speck of light marked where Uncle Ben was working away in the loft over the stable.

They turned and rode slowly down into the

valley. And as they rode, Freddy slung his guitar around and after a preliminary twangle, struck into the song that they had sung on the road to Florida, so many years ago.

"Oh, the sailor may sing of his tall, swift ships,
  Of sailing the deep blue sea,
But the long, long road where adventure waits
  Is the better life for me.

Not the broad highroad that runs dead straight,
  With never a loop nor bend,
But the narrow road, the gypsy road—
  The road that has no end.

The road of adventure's the gypsy road,
  Where ghosts and goblins lurk,
Where rounding a curve you may see tall towers,
  Or a sign saying "Dwarves at Work."

Each one would sing a verse, while the others hummed an accompaniment. Sometimes it was a brand new verse, composed on the spur of the moment, or if the singer couldn't think of anything, he repeated a verse from the old song, which by now had nearly a hundred verses. Then they would join in on the chorus, which went like this:

"Oh, the winding road is long, is long,
  But never too long for me.
And we'll cheer each mile with a song, a song,
A song as we ramble along, along,
  So fearless and gay and free."

Cy was the only one who didn't sing. He had tried a few times, but the other animals always asked him to stop. Most horses are poor singers. It isn't so much that they can't carry a tune, as that they carry it off into a tuneless screeching where nobody could follow them, even if he wanted to. That left only Jinx, Bill, and Freddy.

Their voices blended pleasantly, but on the second chorus, Freddy thought he heard a fourth voice, softly singing a very capable, deep bass. He listened carefully. It was not Jinx, whose high wailing tenor was easy to distinguish. Nor was it Bill, whose baritone was true, but a good deal like a bleat. He glanced at Cy, but the horse's mouth was closed.

The bass accompaniment grew louder. It was a fine, true tone, and gave some unexpected, but very pleasing twists to the harmony. Then suddenly Freddy looked around. And there was Samuel Jackson, his head sticking out of the saddlebag, his mouth wide open as he reached

for a deep one. "Well, for goodness' sake!" said
Freddy.

He nodded encouragingly at Samuel. "Your
verse," he said.

And Samuel sang:

> *"Or a fleet of saucers from far-off Mars*
> *Coasting in for a landing,*
> *Or a group of animals from the farm*
> *With Frederick Bean commanding."*

The others all turned and stared at the mole,
and it wasn't until he had started the second line
that they resumed their humming accompaniment. Then they stood still, all facing Samuel,
as they sang the chorus.

Then they began congratulating him. "Hey,"
said Jinx, "why didn't you tell us you could sing
like that?"

"You must have had a lot of lessons," said Bill.

"All moles can sing," said Samuel. "And I did
tell you. I say I did tell you. When I asked if I
could go on the trip, I said I had a lot of songs
and stories. But you never asked me any more
about them."

The animals looked a little embarrassed, and
after a minute Freddy said: "You see, Samuel,
we don't know much about moles. We hardly

ever see one. Did you know moles could sing, Jinx?"

"Didn't know anything about them," said the cat.

"Trouble with you barnyard animals," said Samuel, "you don't know much of anything about what goes on outside your own little circle. Cows and pigs and dogs and horses and chickens and goats—you just got a tight little club here, and folks that ain't in it, you just don't know that they exist. Take us moles singing. When we aren't hunting, about all we do is get together and sing. There isn't anything else to do underground in the evening. Our eyes aren't very good, and so we don't care to go sight-seeing. We've been singing here for a hundred years or more, and I bet you there isn't an animal on this farm that even knows we're here."

"I don't see how you can blame us for that," said Bill. "If we don't see you and we don't hear you, how could we know?"

"Maybe you're right," said Samuel. "But after I told you—well, you didn't seem very anxious to have me go along on this trip. You just think because you never knew a mole before, that he won't be good company."

"Look, Samuel," said Freddy, "if we really

hadn't wanted you, we wouldn't have let you come. We're glad to have you with us. And, I'll admit, we're doubly glad when we know you have such a fine voice, because we like to sing, too. Is that right, animals?"

"Sure," they said. "Sure." And they all went up and shook hands with Samuel and congratulated him.

"O.K.," said Freddy. "Now let's get going. And have another song. How about "Down By the Old Mill Stream"? Got a good bass for that, Samuel?"

"Try me," said the mole.

So Freddy started. "Down by the—" And the others came in: "—old mill stre-e-eam. Where I first met you-u-u—"

Samuel's bass was magnificent. "Golly," Freddy thought, "we've got a full quartet now. We can give concerts and probably pay all the expenses of the trip." He turned and looked at Jinx with raised eyebrows (of course they were the painted gypsy ones that hadn't been scrubbed off yet). And Jinx winked and nodded, and raised clasped forepaws above his head and shook them.

And so they went on, singing song after song, up around the east end of Otesaraga Lake. It got to be two o'clock, and three. Lights went on in lonely farmhouse windows, and heads were poked out, wondering where the lovely music was coming from. Deer and rabbits and wood-chucks raised their heads to listen, and even por-cupines, who are not a musical race, grunted appreciation.

But at last Freddy said he guessed they'd better get a little sleep. So they found a sheltered spot in a fence corner, and then they sang "Good Night, Ladies." And when they'd all lain down and squirmed around until they were comfort-able, Samuel sang a lullaby. He sang very softly, and by the time he reached the end of the second verse the others were sound asleep. So Samuel curled up in the saddlebag and closed his eyes and smiled happily. "Now," he thought, "I'm one of the gang."

APR   2010